KALAK OF THE ICE

Jim Kjelgaard

KALAK
OF THE ICE

ILLUSTRATED BY BOB KUHN

CONTENTS

KALAK OF THE ICE

Chapter I

THE BAY OF SEALS

The wind, blowing in from the sea, rippled the water where pack and shore ice parted. From the air, the open water resembled an irregular river in the ice.

A lone white gull hovered over the open lead, and looked with bright eyes at the water below. He banked, and flew slowly up the lead with bent head. The gull squawked querulously, crossed the lead, and reversed his direction.

Suddenly the gull planed down toward the open water. Then, within inches of the surface, he flapped upward again. From the height at which he had

flown, a floating chip of ice had looked like a dead
fish. Not often was the gull guilty of such error. But
now he could afford to miss no opportunity to get
food. His last meal, a few shrimp, had been eaten
twenty hours ago. Desperate hunger prodded the
bird.

The gull wheeled again, and patiently started back
up that side of the lead which he had already explor-
ed. Suddenly he dived, hovered for a second over the
water, and snatched and gulped a small fish that floated belly-up. The gull came to rest on an ice hummock, folded his wings, and moved his bill as though
he were still savoring the tiny fish. The morsel had
merely dulled the sharpest edge of the gull's appetite,
but that was something.

Rested, the gull took wing and flew swiftly out
over the ice pack, head bent as he scanned the ice
beneath him. His objective was another open lead,
where shrimp might come to the surface or where he
might find another dead fish. Suddenly the gull wheeled and swung back over the ice. So perfectly did the
animals below him blend with their surroundings that
he had almost passed without seeing them.

He had to look sharply when he returned, but now
he could see the two polar bears on the pack ice. The

gull settled on an ice hummock a few yards from them, and folded his wings. He knew now that he would eat. Sooner or later the bears would make a kill.

The gull waited patiently.

Kalak, the she polar bear, and her yearling cub had been out on the pack. Living on the ice, sleeping there when they were tired, eating the seals that appeared wherever there was an open lead, they had not been near land since the long winter night lifted and the sun shone once more. But now, with the approach of summer, they were ranging back toward land.

As they approached the shore, Kalak was cautious and fretful, quartering to catch in her nostrils any stray gust that might bring a message from land. However, the wind carried no evidence of either food or danger.

The bear saw the gull come down, but paid no attention to it. Usually, in summer, there were one or more gulls about to feed on the remains of her kills. Kalak did not mind as long as the gulls were not impudent and did not try to feed while she and the cub were eating. Her present problem, like the gull's, was to find something to eat.

Yesterday, far out on the ice, Kalak and the cub had

fed on a fat seal. Then they had lain down to sleep before travelling on under the light of the midnight sun.
A few hours ago they had started to hunt again, and
now were very hungry.

The cub was fretful, but Kalak had been hungry
before. She knew that if she kept travelling, sooner or
later she would find something to eat. Frequently, in
her previous experience, she had run across places
where, because a strong current had swept the shrimp
away or there was no current to bring them in, there
were no shrimp. And she knew that the seals upon
which she lived were not to be found where there was
not an abundance of shrimp or fish for them to eat.

Kalak and the cub swam the open lead and climbed
out on the short ice. Sometimes dead whales—either
small white whales or the mighty bowheads—washed
up on shore and furnished food in plenty. Kalak strode
on, head extended and nostrils flaring to catch any
scent that might rise. But nothing had travelled here
recently enough to leave a scent.

The cub, growing more and more irritable as hunger pinched, padded up beside Kalak and grunted.

The mother bear swung her head to bunt the cub
and knock him sprawling. She, too, had become irritable. Hunger had not made her so; she had just wea-

ried of the cub's complaining. Then, too, the wind from the sea had lulled, and with no wind to brush the ice and carry its cold touch to the shore, all the heat generated by a constantly shining sun had become oppressive.

Kalak turned again to vent her displeasure on the cub. Turning so hastily that he almost somersaulted backward, the cub ran a few yards and stood looking over his shoulder to see what was going to happen next. Kalak grunted sourly, and turned back to the sea. The cub followed at a safe distance.

Their hindquarters submerged, swimming only with their front paws, they surged back across the open lead and climbed out among the broken hummocks and ridges on the pack ice. As the bears threaded their expert way among them, the gull took flight and flew in slow circles high above them.

Kalak and the cub came to open water. The wind had increased, and before them waves rolled and fell back in whitecaps. There was a sudden shuddering crack as the chunk of ice on which the bears stood broke off and, pushed by the wind, started toward the dimly seen ice pack on the far side of the open water. For a while the bears rode their raft. Then they slipped easily into the water and started swimming. In a few minutes the drifting ice cake was left far behind.

When they reached the far side, Kalak climbed out on the pack ice and waited for the cub to join her. As he did so, the eddying wind brought the faint scent of basking seals. The cub, too, caught the scent and padded eagerly forward, whining softly. Kalak let him go. In the near future he would have to hunt for himself, and earn his own way in this land of ice, just as she always had. He must learn to hunt by hunting.

After he had taken the lead, Kalak followed him quietly. Her big padded paws made no noise on the ice; she was careful to keep away from hummocks and ridges from which ice might break and alarm the seal. She watched the cub's progress·critically.

The scent of open water came from just ahead, and with it was mingled,the distinct odor of a near-by seal. The cub sank down, flattening himself on the ice and pushing noiselessly forward with groping hind feet. Kalak crawled behind him, around one·last·hummock, and saw the seal sunning himself almost at the very edge of a wide lead. Kalak stopped, but the cub went on, all his eager interest centered on the prey he was trying to stalk.

The seal raised its head to look about. The cub stopped, freezing where he was. The seal lowered his head. When it did so, the cub pushed himself forward.

Then the cub let anxiety overcome judgment. Rather than stop when the seal raised its head again, he continued his stalk. Although almost invisible against the ice, so well did his coat blend with it, he was still seen by the experienced seal. For a bare second the seal stared at the moving white object. Then, as though he were on a greased chute, the seal slid into the water and dived under the protecting ice.

The disgust she felt evident in every line of her body, Kalak rose and strode to the still-crouched cub. She raised an immense front paw, and delivered a blow that sent the cub skidding across the ice. Kalak did not look back, but this time she led while the cub followed meekly.

The bear's nose soon told her that there were more seals ahead. She stopped, flattened on the ice, and pushed herself around an ice hummock. Twenty feet away, down an icy incline, there was another open lead. On the far side, near enough to the water so that it could slide instantly to safety, another seal basked in the sun.

Kalak backed carefully behind the hummock, and crawled on a line parallel with the lead, until she was a hundred yards from a point opposite the seal. When she started toward the water again, Kalak grunted meaningly. The chastised cub remained where he was.

Slowly, with infinite patience, the mother bear worked her way toward the lead, her eyes on the seal. Every time it raised its head, or even stirred, Kalak froze where she was. When she finally reached the water, she slid her great bulk into it so quietly that scarcely a spreading ripple revealed her presence. With only her nose protruding, she swam slowly toward the seal. The cub and the circling gull saw the basking animal raise its head and stay alert. Kalak, the most expert of hunters, had made no noise, but still the seal sensed danger. It slid toward the water.

But when the seal reached it, Kalak was there. She had marked the place exactly, and received the two-hundred-pound seal squarely in her jaws. Clinging to the ice with her front paws, she clamped her teeth tightly until the seal stopped thrashing.

As easily as a terrier carries a rat, Kalak carried her prey out on the ice. The eager cub rose, ran to the water, scrambled in, and swam across. There on the bleak ice Kalak and her cub feasted on the hapless seal's rich blubber. Surfeited, they sought a near-by hummock and lay down to sleep beside it.

The hungry gull swooped down beside the remains of the seal.

Four hours later, Kalak and her cub arose, yawning and stretching. Propped up on her front paws, like an immense dog, Kalak read the stories the wind brought to her. Then side by side, the bears started off across the pack ice.

They swam leads where they found them, drank from fresh-water lakes formed where old salt ice had freshened and melted and, when they wanted to rest, lay in the shaded portions of ice hummocks or ridges.

The next day, Kalak caught another seal. There was not an abundance of them here, but there were more than there had been in the coastal area patrolled by the lonely gull. Nearly every lead held a few shrimp and, beneath the ice, there were fish ranging in size from small herring to great cod.

Kalak's route kept her almost along the line where the pack ice ground against the frozen shore. It was a rugged journey which in turn led over smooth ice, across old ice whose humps and ridges had melted until it resembled a frozen prairie, over ice still humped in sixty-foot ridges and crests, and across open sea.

The two polar bears took all of it in their stride, catching seals where they needed them and resting when rest was called for. They did not swerve from their path, even when the ice about them churned and broke, and heaped itself in still higher ridges. This was Kalak's country; she was as much at home in it as any land beast can be in its own domain. She knew and understood the ice pack as well as the moose knows and understands his forest, or the bighorn his crags.

The difference between the sea ice and the land lay in the fact that the ice was an ever-changing world. There were no paths which might be the same next year or even next day. The pack always moved and, in moving, opened new water where none had been or closed leads that were open. Kalak found her way because of a deep-seated intelligence in her brain and a compass in her nose. So she took her cub where she willed and always found the best path to go there.

On their third day of travel, Kalak stopped suddenly. She inched behind a hummock, and stood as still as the ice beside her. The cub, coming up behind her, stopped too. Every tiny nerve in Kalak's immense body was alert as she sought a repetition of the thing that had halted her in her tracks.

It came again. From across the ice, in the direction of the shore, there floated the far-off barking of a dog.

The dog barked still again, and another joined in. The cub moved slightly, crumbling the ice beneath him. Kalak whirled furiously upon him, and the cub backed to the hummock and stood still.

Kalak waited as only a wild creature could wait, one who had learned the certain value of patience and caution. Although her ears had warned her first, she was waiting for the full knowledge that only her nose could supply. But the wind was keening in from the sea, in the wrong direction. Neither she nor the cub moved a muscle.

Then the wind eddied, and momentarily came rolling back from shore. In that moment Kalak learned all that she wished to know.

It was a familiar odor, that of the Endorah Eskimo village. Mingled with the scent of humans was that of many dogs, but not as many as there had been the last time Kalak had come within scenting distance of the village. There was also the odor of skin tents, the stench that always gathers around a camp, the rich smell of seal oil, and the smell of driftwood fires. The big ice bear stood perfectly still, making up her mind what to do. She was afraid.

It was not fear for herself. Steel-muscled and sinewed, equipped with pile-driver paws and jaws that were capable of breaking a seal's back with one bite, she knew and understood her own strength and hardihood. She was experienced and cunning, or else she would have died long ago. The arctic shores and the polar pack were no place for weaklings. Kalak had never been afraid for herself.

But deep within her lay something that was entirely separate from savagery and brute force. She must hunt, and fight, and run if need be, so that her young might survive. That was irresistible instinct, but an instinct sharpened in her case by bitter memories. Kalak had a great capacity for loving her cub, and was worried because she knew of the many dangers that could strike down her young.

The first time she had become a mother, young and inexperienced, she had left her two cubs to go seal hunting. She had not remained away for long, but when she returned the cubs were gone, blood stained the den, and there was the scent of wolves about. Then she had again borne twin cubs, and seen them run down by a sputtering launch that was lowered from the deck of a great ship. Kalak had tried to rescue them, but the launch was swifter than she and it had drawn rapidly away. For days she had roamed the sea, furiously striking at anything that lay in her path and not eating as she sought her kidnapped young. She had never found them. The next time she had borne only one cub, and had seen him crushed by a collapsing wall of ice.

Now again she had but one cub upon which she could lavish all her love. The cub had been at her side for more than a year, and Kalak had kept him out on the ice pack partly because she knew that hunters from the Eskimo village seldom ventured that far. She was not afraid of the hunters, but she was terribly afraid of the harm they might bring to her cub. She could go back to the ice pack, but hunting would be poor there at this time of year.

Wheeling, Kalak loped swiftly away from the dangerous scent and led the cub swiftly out on the ice pack. Coming to a lead, they plunged in and swam across. The two bears had not eaten for many hours and were hungry. But despite the protesting whimpers of the cub, Kalak did not stop to hunt even when the odor of near-by seals was borne to her nostrils.

When, at last, Kalak turned again to face the shore and wait for the changing wind to bring her the story of what lay there, she found no taint of man. There was only the clean smell of the pack in the cold wind that blew into her receptive nostrils. Kalak slowed her pace, and swung back in the direction she had been travelling when she smelled the Eskimo village. The cub whimpered again, plaintively, and this time his mother did not rebuff him. Kalak stopped to hunt.

The next day they came to a great area of open water and stood on the edge of the pack while they stared across its apparently endless expanse.

Directly before them, half a hundred yards from the shore, a gam of bowhead whales floated near the surface and sent their water spouts high into the air. The cub watched with his head up, eyes and ears alert, and padded down to the very edge of the ice so he could see better. He reared himself to his full height. A throaty growl bubbled from his cub throat as, in every way a polar bear can, he challenged the whales to come in and fight.

Suddenly the edge of the ice cracked, slid into the sea, and took the cub with it. He tumbled in headfirst and heels in the air. Then, just as he was about to strike the water, he straightened himself out and dived cleanly. The cub surfaced, swam back to the ice, and clawed his way up onto it. He looked sheepishly at Kalak, then walked back to the ice's edge, being careful not to go too near, and growled again at the whales.

Kalak swung along the edge of the ice, and followed it mile after mile. In late afternoon they came upon creatures that had climbed out of the sea to the ice.
The cub pushed eagerly ahead to look at them. Huge
beasts with long ivory tusks, they were even bigger
than Kalak. This time the cub did not growl, but looked questioningly at his mother. The herd of walrus was too near; if he challenged them to battle they
might accept. The walrus only raised their heads and
stared when the polar bears went by.

In mid-morning of the sixth day they came to the
Bay of Seals.

The Bay itself was merely a great indentation in the
arctic coast. Shore ice, accumulated over the years,
had crawled far up on the slate rocks that stretched
away from the sea. A strong north wind was blowing
and the restless pack ice ground against the shore.
Farther out, the Bay was solid ice, split at various
places by leads of differing widths. Seals almost without number crowded the edges of the leads, or hunted
shrimp in the open water.

The Bay of Seals was a wild and lonely place. It was
a lost world in itself, a savage and storm-lashed spot
that could be visited only by the hardiest and most
daring of arctic hunters. But the shrimp and fish that

swarmed in the open leads or beneath the ice attracted the seals, and, in summer, many polar bears came to feed on the seals.

From where she stood Kalak saw thirteen of the great ice bears, and the wind brought her the scent of many more. The cub, dismayed at finding himself among so many of his kind, crowded close at his mother's heels.

A huge bear with a snake-like head and lean body emerged from the water, stood beside the lead from which he had climbed, and looked silently at Kalak and her cub. Kalak lowered her head and bared yellow tushes, while a rumbling threat issued from her throat. The male bear dived back into the lead and swam across.

At this display of his mother's invincibility, the cub strode cockily forward. Kalak walked at his side, missing nothing, particularly aware of anything that might threaten the cub.

A summer fog began to settle over the Bay. Its curling tendrils slowly obscured the ice, the shore, and the open leads. The wind died, but the breezes still carried the scent of those living creatures which were abroad in the bay. As Kalak strode swiftly forward, the cub remained close at her heels.

Out of the mist loomed a white presence, a thing that was more sensed than seen. Kalak did not break her pace, but the cub cringed against her when he saw the beast that had come. It was a monstrous bear, a creature bigger than Kalak. This time the cub's mother did not growl when the bigger bear approached.

Thus, in a blinding mist over the Bay of Seals, Kalak met the far-ranging mate whom she had not seen since winter last closed over the ice fields.

Chapter II

HUNGRY VILLAGE

Agtuk, Chief of the Endorah Eskimos, was very tired. When yesterday's sun had shone over the ice pack he had started back into the hills to hunt caribou. Since then he had slept not at all, though Toolah and Nalee, the only two hunters who had dared travel with him, had lain on a sunny hill and slumbered. Agtuk was also angry. There were other men back in the village capable of hunting, but instead of getting out and searching for game they preferred to sit in the council house and let Chuesandrin, the devil-driver, tell them why they couldn't get it.

The devil had control, Chuesandrin said, and all

the magic he could muster was of no avail because the devil abode among them in the body of Agtuk's favorite dog, Natkus. The devil would not depart, nor would game be plentiful, until Agtuk thrust Chuesandrin's magic knife through Natkus' heart. And most of the tribe believed it.

Agtuk fingered his own knife. He had never killed any man because he considered that the killing of men was not right, but he thought that he would not mind killing Chuesandrin. He knew that the devil-driver had been smoldering for more than two months, ever since Natkus had entered his tent and stolen a choice caribou loin that Chuesandrin's wife was roasting. Agtuk's mouth tightened.

One did not, of course, take even a favorite dog along when one hunted caribou because dogs frightened them. But before leaving the village Agtuk had told Chuesandrin that Natkus had best be present when Agtuk returned. If he were not, Agtuk had said, then Chuesandrin would not be present for very long either. Natkus was not to go into the cooking pots, where so many of the village dogs had already gone, nor was he to be subjected to any of Chuesandrin's devil-driving.

Agtuk had made himself very clear. He did not, he

said, believe that Chuesandrin knew any more about devils than anyone else, or even that there was a devil. Agtuk had lived for thirty-nine years among the Endorah. More than once he had seen a scarcity of game, and more than once, even when there had been no devil-driver to lure it back, the game had returned. If Chuesandrin cared to put the issue to a test, then Agtuk would gladly submit. They would see which was the stronger, Chuesandrin's magic or Agtuk's knife. It was time a decision was reached.

As Agtuk squatted on the small hill he had climbed, and thought about these things, he squinted across the treeless country that rolled away from the hill. There was no game in sight, and Agtuk was worried. If they did not find meat soon the whole village would starve. As it was, they had been able to get just enough to maintain strength. Everybody except the children and the old people were hungry most of the time.

Toolah and Nalee came up beside him, laid their spears and their bows and arrows on the ground, and stared down the hill. For a moment no one spoke.

"This is a bad thing," Toolah said.

"It is not good," Agtuk agreed.

"Perhaps," Toolah said thoughtfully, "there really is a devil keeping the game away. Perhaps if you did as

Chuesandrin wishes, and killed Natkus with his magic knife—"

"Chuesandrin babbles child's talk for children's ears," Agtuk said sourly.

Toolah did not answer for a moment, and then he said hesitantly, "Perhaps so."

Agtuk said, still sourly, "Those who wish to eat may put their trust in devil-drivers or hunting. Those who hunt will eat."

"We have found nothing to hunt," Nalee pointed out.

"That is so," Agtuk agreed, "but we must continue to search. Since we did not get any caribou we will go out on the ice and try again for seals. If there are no seals, we will look for something else. I shall give a spear to both Toolah and Nalee."

The hunters' leathery faces brightened. Aside from being the best and most skillful hunter, Agtuk was far and away the finest spear-maker in the tribe. It was no small honor to own one of his spears; only the greatest hunters had them, and the prospect of one was sufficient to balance Chuesandrin's devils. Nalee and Toolah nodded agreeably. They would continue to hunt with Agtuk.

Agtuk rose. "There is no use in staying here and

wasting time. We might as well return to the village and set out on a seal hunt."

They started toward the river where they had left their kayaks. Sweat beaded their foreheads, for the day was hot. With his knife Agtuk opened a worn place in the front of his fawn-skin shirt. Ostensibly the move was calculated to cool his body, but it was also a bold gesture which Nalee and Toolah did not miss. Anyone who became so reckless with caribou-skin garments must be sure that he would get more.

As they mounted a hill, overlooking the willow-lined river, Agtuk sank quickly behind the crest of the rise. Toolah and Nalee, behind him, also crouched down. Agtuk turned to them.

"There are two bull caribou across the river. We must get them!"

"Let us be on, then," Toolah said eagerly.

Agtuk shook his head.

"We cannot hunt as though there are plenty of caribou if we miss these. We must plan carefully."

"No hunting plan is certain," Nalee argued.

"This one must be sure," Agtuk said. "You, Toolah, and you, Nalee, go back to the bottom of the hill and work your way downstream. Be careful that the caribou do not see you and take fright. When you have come to the shallow part, wade across the river and go far enough back so that you are behind the caribou. Then come in, toward the river. If you can, kill both bulls with arrows. If you cannot, drive them so that they will enter the river when they flee. I will be waiting by the willows, and when they are in the water I will try to overtake them in my kayak."

"It is a good plan." Toolah's eyes were filled with admiration.

"A hunter's plan," Nalee agreed. "We go."

The two left, and Agtuk crawled back to the crest of the hill. The two bulls were still feeding on the other side of the river. While they fed, Agtuk crawled carefully down the hill. When the caribou ceased feeding and raised their heads, Agtuk stopped and held himself perfectly motionless. When the caribou resumed their feeding again, Agtuk crawled on. He knew that caribou thought nothing was dangerous unless it was in motion, and they were too far away to smell him.

By slow degrees Agtuk reached the willow-lined river bank, and the kayak he had hidden there. Now there was nothing to do except wait, but Agtuk was a hunter born to hunting. He knew well the value of patience and of doing the right thing at the right time. With his eye Agtuk measured the distance to the kayak and noted the exact location of the paddle. When the time came to act, it would need to be swift action. He would have no time for waste motions.

For an hour, moving only far enough to find the choicest browse, the caribou fed, undisturbed. Then, both bulls raised their heads suddenly and glanced behind them. They made a nervous little start, and ran a few feet. Agtuk saw Nalee rise up and shoot an arrow. But it was hopelessly far shooting, and the arrow fell short. Both bulls started to run.

Agtuk waited, holding his breath. Instead of coming down to the river, the caribou were heading upstream, along the bank. Agtuk muttered to himself. Where was Toolah? If Toolah and Nalee missed, they should at least be in a position to force the bulls into the river.

One of the caribou stopped, whirled, and dashed directly away from the river, toward the low hills. Toolah rose out of the grass, with drawn bow, but his arrow soared over the bull's back. Agtuk muttered again.

Seeing Toolah, the second bull took the opposite direction, raced toward the river, and plunged in.

Agtuk made no move; if he launched his kayak now he might drive the caribou back to the opposite bank.

With an expert eye he gauged its progress. The caribou, coming to deep water, stopped splashing and started to swim strongly. It was almost in the center of the river when Agtuk pushed his kayak into the water.

He paddled swiftly, sending the frail craft through the water so fast that a trailing wake curled from its stern. Seeing him, but still intent upon gaining the shore toward which it had started, the bull swerved upstream. Agtuk drove his paddle deeper, putting into his strokes all the strength of his powerful arms. Slowly he closed the gap between himself and the swimming caribou.

Then, with a rending snap that sounded very loud above the river's placid murmur, his paddle split. The kayak lost headway.

Agtuk threw his spear. It was a long cast, but expertly done. The spear soared in a long arc to bite into the swimming bull's flank.

Agtuk began propelling the kayak forward with what remained of the paddle. He could not go as fast, but the spear had penetrated far enough to impede the swimming bull seriously. For a moment it continued its desperate efforts to fight upstream, then quartered across. It had almost reached the shallows on the side of the river when Agtuk brought his kayak alongside, and flung himself out of it to land squarely astride the swimming bull's back.

The bull's head came up and his antlers snapped back toward the man's ribs. Agtuk wound his left hand in the caribou's hair, crouched as low as he could get on the bull's back, and brought up his knife with his right hand. He thrust it down with a mighty stroke that sent the blade out of sight in the bull's chest. The caribou kicked and thrashed furiously for a moment, but Agtuk's thrust had been sure. In a moment the bull was floating quietly.

As soon as Agtuk had thrown himself on the bull, Toolah and Nalee had started running for the shallow ford across the river. They now came panting up to where they had left their kayaks, howling with delight.

"A caribou!" Toolah yelled. "A bull falls before Agtuk! There will be meat in the cooking pots tonight!"

They launched their own kayaks, retrieved Agtuk's, and helped him secure the bull with a sealskin thong. As they towed it to shore, Toolah drew his knife, made a slash in the air, held the knife to his lips, and grinned broadly. "Agtuk the hunter!" he crowed. "Let Chuesandrin's devils match this!"

They drew the bull up on the bank, and began to dress it.

"The very grandfather of all caribou," Agtuk observed wryly. "Its flesh all but turns my knife blade."

"It is not the tenderest," Nalee agreed, "but it is meat."

Agtuk sliced the raw liver, gave chunks of it to Toolah and Nalee, and they all sat down to eat. Finished, although still hungry, Agtuk stared thoughtfully toward the rolling hills in which the remaining bull had made good his escape. Then he addressed Toolah and Nalee.

"Take the meat down to the village," he directed. "I stay here."

Toolah looked quizzically at him.

"But why?"

"To hunt the bull we did not get," Agtuk said simply. "The village is in need."

"You will be honored for getting this one," Toolah objected.

"Honor," Agtuk observed, "is not enough when my people need food. I stay here."

He picked up an axe, expertly chopped around the dead bull's scalp and lifted the antlers from it. With his knife he cut a long strip of skin and tied one end to the antlers. Then he made a loop in the other end of the thong and slung the antlers over his shoulder. He picked up his bow and arrows, and the spear that had been taken out of the dead bull. Toolah and Nalee waited questioningly. Agtuk took a small chunk of meat for himself and dropped it into his kayak.

"Go!" he urged. "The village is hungry!"

Without looking back he paddled across the river, beached his kayak, and started out on the trail of the bull that had escaped.

The sun beat mercilessly down and Agtuk sweated profusely. The dangling antlers butted his thigh, and he shifted them to the other shoulder. When he had gone half a mile he climbed a hill to look. There was nothing in sight, but he had not really expected anything; frightened caribou ran for very long distances before they even stopped to graze. Agtuk lay down, pillowed his head on a rock, and slept for an hour. Then he patiently took up the dim trail left by the running bull.

He knew where to go partly because of the bull's faint tracks and partly because he knew caribou. There were places where they might be expected to travel and other places which they most certainly would avoid, and anyone who hoped successfully to hunt must be able to guess what his game would do. Agtuk pressed on under the never-setting sun.

A single cloud appeared in the sky, and hung ominously there. Other clouds joined it, and their shadows began to shroud the treeless hills across which the lone bull had trotted. Agtuk started to run along the trail.

The desperate village needed all the food it could get, and he dared not miss this bull if there was a possibility of getting it. However, the wind that keened in from the sea carried cold with it and the clouds meant snow. If snow fell there would be no chance to find the lone bull.

When he could run no longer, Agtuk walked until his spent breath was recovered, then trotted on again. It was the next day when he finally sighted the caribou, grazing in a valley between two hills.

Agtuk knelt in the grass, unslung the caribou antlers, and used the thong with which he had carried them to strap the antlers to his back. Without attempting to conceal himself, he crawled openly down the hill. The bull saw him, raised its head, and resumed grazing. It did not run and showed no sign of fear. Agtuk continued his steady crawl, dragging his bow with one hand. As he came nearer, the caribou stared stead-

ily at him. Then, its short tail high, the bull came forward. Agtuk stopped, and nocked an arrow in his bow.

A sudden blast of wind, the beginning of the storm,
roared across the low hills. Blowing from Agtuk to the
caribou, it carried man scent to the bull. The caribou
whirled and loped away. As it disappeared over the
rise, snow started to fall.

Wearily, Agtuk turned and started his long home-
ward journey.

The village, a collection of skin-covered tents, stood
on the shore where the river met the arctic sea. As far
out as Agtuk could see, the flowing river had eaten its
way into the pack ice, so there was open sea in front of
the camp. Farther out, where Kalak and her cub had
crossed, the river's ice-cooled water at last flowed ineffectively against more pack ice.

Agtuk beached his kayak, and strode up the bank
to greet the woman who waited for him there. Larensa, his capable wife, smiled in return.

"You have returned in good time, Agtuk," she said.

"Empty-handed," he replied grimly. "Is all well in
the village?"

"Thanks to the hunting skill of Agtuk, there is some
meat."

"And Natkus . . . ?"

A big gray dog with a lithe wolf's body tore across the village. He flung himself upon Agtuk, whimpering and wagging his tail furiously. Larensa watched understandingly. She lived in a harsh land where the only possible means of life lay in hunting. It was good to see the hunter reunited with his dog, for that meant that there would be more hunting and more food. Larensa smiled.

"Natkus has grieved since you left," she said. "He also chased Chuesandrin across the village, and I think he would have bitten him had not Chuesandrin gained the safety of his house."

"Oh," said Agtuk, "and what has the great devil-driver been doing?"

Larensa shook her head dubiously. "He gives all his time to the making of magic, Agtuk. He has become even more bitter toward Natkus. I think that the evil things stirring in the devil-driver's mind now extend to the master of Natkus."

"How does the village think?"

"Some side with you, since Toolah and Nalee brought in the caribou meat. Some are still afraid of Chuesandrin. I fear there will be bad times."

Agtuk said shortly, "I go to see Chuesandrin."

With Natkus at his heels he strode across the village to the devil-driver's tent, and went in without announcing his presence.

Chuesandrin, who had blackened his face, was bending over a seal-oil lamp from which yellow flame rose. Without looking up, the devil-driver passed his hand over the flame. It turned red, then turned pure white. Still Chuesandrin did not look up. Agtuk watched calmly.

"You are wasting your talents upon me, Chuesandrin. I know all about the stones and dust you may gather, that will make a lamp burn almost any color you wish when you conceal some in the palm of your hand and drop it in."

Natkus pushed in beside Agtuk, and growled softly. Chuesandrin glanced up. His eyes were fanatically alight, his voice was a harsh whisper.

"The dog!" he croaked. "The dog in which the devil lives!" He extended a knife. "Thrust it in the dog now and kill the devil! There will be no game until you do!"

Agtuk spoke harshly. "I am tired, Chuesandrin, for I have been hunting while you have been here frightening villagers who are already frightened enough. I do not mind your making magic, for our people have always had devil-drivers among them. But I do think it is time you foresaw the return of game, and thus put heart in the hunters to get out and work for themselves!"

"There will be no game!" the devil-driver said. "There will be none until you kill the devil in your dog!"

Agtuk said contemptuously, "I heard that Natkus tried to bite you, Chuesandrin. It is too bad that he did not succeed, for had Natkus eaten a good meal of devil-driver I would not have to feed him other meat. I go now, but I leave you with the hope that you change both your ways and your devil-driving. There would be enough food for all if enough hunters looked for it."

With Natkus behind him, Agtuk swung on his heel and left the devil-driver's tent. Coming toward him were Toolah and Nalee, flanked by four other men. Toolah spoke happily.

"Nalee and I have been to your lodge, Agtuk. True to your promise, Larensa gave each of us a hunting spear made by you. Here are others who are now willing to hunt."

"It is not that we wish to offend Chuesandrin," a stocky hunter said hesitantly. "It is just that Toolah and Nalee came to no harm by hunting with you. We will hunt if you will promise to give us spears, too."

Agtuk reflected. If sufficient hunters went out, enough food might be had. And if he had not sufficient spears to give a weapon to everyone who helped bring game down, he could make some more. If the magic of owning a spear made by Agtuk counteracted the magic Chuesandrin brewed in his devil-driver's tent . . .

"It is good," Agtuk said. "We will hunt, then. And now is the time to start! Look!"

His glance had strayed out across the open water. Far out, so far that it was seen only faintly, a spout of water ascended toward the sky and fell back. The spout appeared again.

"Whale!" Agtuk shouted. "Be quick!"

Agtuk ran to his tent and snatched up his seven-foot whaling harpoon and his twelve-foot lance. The harpoon had a slate head, to which was attached a sixty-foot walrus-hide line. On the end of the line were three floats, each made by inflating the skin of an entire seal.

Carrying his whaling gear, Agtuk ran down to the beach where an oomiak, a large boat covered with walrus hide, was always ready to launch. Toolah, Nalee, and the other four hunters appeared, each carrying similar weapons. They launched the oomiak, caught up paddles, and sent the big boat skimming lightly over the calm sea. Agtuk, in the bow, rested his harpoon in the built-in ivory launching crotch.

But the sea upon which the whale had been sighted was now calm and deserted. The paddlers swung the oomiak and quartered to cover that section which they had not yet been over. They came to the pack ice, so far out that no land was visible, and started back.

Suddenly, completely without warning, the whale came up within a few feet of the oomiak.

It was an old whale, a great forbidding monster more than sixty-five feet long from the tip of its nose to the end of its tail. The whale moved sluggishly, and sent up another water spout whose spray blew down over the oomiak from high in the air.

Agtuk hurled his weapon, and saw the harpoon's head bury itself in the whale's thick hide. As the sluggish monster sounded, the shaft tore loose from the harpoon's head and floated free. The whaling line played over the oomiak's edge so fast that a little column of smoke rose, and the floats followed the sounding whale out of sight.

Toolah passed his harpoon to Agtuk, who rested it

in the launching fork while the hunters waited tensely. A whale was a great creature from which tons of meat could be cut. If they were able to get this one, then the village would have plenty of food, and oil and blubber for their lamps. Agtuk's would be a village of plenty.

The hunters waited for the floats on the whaling line to bring the monster back to the surface. When he came, another harpoon with more floats would be hurled. Eventually, with the floats holding him back, the whale would be unable to submerge. Then he could be dispatched at close quarters with the razor-sharp lances.

"There he is!"

The eager cry broke from Nalee. Two hundred yards to the left, the sealskin floats bobbed to the surface. Swinging their oomiak, the paddlers worked so furiously that the bow of their craft was lifted out of the water. Agtuk made ready to hurl another harpoon.

Then, as one man, the paddlers ceased paddling and a disappointed groan arose.

The tough whaling line had broken, and the floats were bobbing freely on the arctic sea. Agtuk reached out to pick them up on the end of his lance, and lifted them into the boat without a word.

As they turned back toward shore, Agtuk pondered. When food was scare it was bad enough to lose a caribou. Losing a whale, enough food to last everyone for months, was indeed a crushing blow. But that was not all. Chuesandrin wished to be master of the village. If he could convince the villagers that devils had anything to do with losing the whale, now was an excellent chance for him to depose Agtuk.

When the oomiak came near, most of the waiting villagers who had crowded the shore to see what the hunters would bring drifted dejectedly back into the village. Only a small group of women, the wives of the hunters who had gone out, remained.

"Ill fortune?" Larensa asked.

"The line broke," Agtuk grunted, as he stepped out of the oomiak.

"Chuesandrin said he knew that you would not get it!" one of the wives said bitterly. "He said the devil in Natkus would prevent your getting anything as great as a whale!"

For a moment Agtuk stood thoughtfully, digesting this information. It was as he had feared. Suddenly he swung on Nalee.

"Tell everyone," he directed, "that I wish to address the village."

Agtuk took his place before the assembled men, women, and children. Even the dogs gathered on the outskirts of the crowd, sensing the excitement. Natkus came to stand by his master's side.

Agtuk looked at Chuesandrin, glowering by himself, and began to speak.

"All of us are hungry and there is not enough food. There will not be enough here. Toolah, Nalee, and I hunted long and hard for one caribou. We must have more. Since the game will not come to us, we must go to the game. We must move."

"Madness!" croaked Chuesandrin. "He talks madness! The devil is keeping the game away, the devil in Agtuk's dog."

Agtuk glanced at Chuesandrin, then continued. "Will you listen to the devil-driver or to a hunter? The game has not disappeared as sea fog melts away! It is merely elsewhere. We must go there. I know a place where there is always game. Let us move to the Bay of Seals!"

"Great madness!" Chuesandrin shrieked. "He knows not whereof he speaks! The Bay of Seals is the abode of many terrible devils!"

"Chuesandrin!" Agtuk replied evenly, "I challenge your power! If you have, as you say you have, any control over devils, then show it now! Have your devils strike me!"

There was a moment of awed silence, while all eyes turned toward Chuesandrin. "If I summoned a devil, Agtuk," he replied, "he would not strike only you. He would strike all."

"Then let him strike all!"

"No! No!" cried several voices.

"You can't!" Agtuk said contemptuously. "What hunters will go with me to the Bay of Seals? Who does not fear?"

Larensa pushed her way through the crowd.

"I will go!" she said clearly. "I am only a woman, but I will go with Agtuk! Will the men of the Endorah dare go where a woman does?"

"I'll go," Nalee called.

"And I," said Toolah. "With my own eyes I saw Agtuk attack a swimming caribou bull and kill it with his knife. I will follow a hunter who can do that!"

"Who else?" Agtuk called. "Who wishes to go with Agtuk and feast, and who prefers to stay with Chuesandrin and starve?"

There was muttering among the villagers as those who wanted to go with Agtuk and those who lived in fear of Chuesandrin's devils argued among themselves. Agtuk waited. Most of the men had swung to his side. Those who had not would follow. Even Chuesandrin would rather sink his teeth into fat seal blubber than remain here and starve. Agtuk had won.

"You, Toolah and Nalee," he ordered, "select five good men to go with us. We shall set out at once, taking our hunting gear and a dog for each man. The rest will follow, and set up our village on the shore of the Bay of Seals."

Chapter III

THE OLD WHALE

The whale had been unaware of the oomiak until Agtuk's harpoon bit into his side.

The whale sounded immediately, fighting the floats which dragged behind him. He was alarmed, but not terrified. Twenty times during the more than hundred years he had prowled the sea he had felt the sting of harpoons, and a dozen heads were still imbedded in his big body.

When the whale reached deeper water he began to tire. The harpoon line strained behind him, the floats exerting more and more pressure as he went deeper. At the bottom the whale turned, beginning to yield to the imperative tug of the sealskin floats. As he turned, the trailing line followed him about a rock abutment buried deep in the sea. Ground for centuries by silt-laden water, the rock's corner was razor-sharp; it cut the harpoon line.

Freed of the dragging floats, the whale spurted forward into still deeper water. He was under the ice now, and the water was black, but still the whale continued to dive. He plumbed the very depths of the ocean, where the water pressure was so intense that a man in a diving suit would have been crushed like an egg shell.

The whale swam swiftly on, and even in the black water, far beneath the ice, he knew where he was. This was an old highway, one whose bends and turns he knew well. The whale was heading toward a place far out in the pack ice where he knew there would be much open water. When he reached it, he ascended to breathe. The imbedded harpoon was only a small ache in his great length, but the whale was very tired. He was old, and had come a long way from the southerly waters where he had passed the winter.

When he moved again he travelled slowly, and frequently turned to go back along the way he followed. He was aimless and restless.

The whale dived. Clearly in the depths to which he had descended he saw a gam of bowhead whales go past, but did not attempt to join them. They meant nothing to him. He was like a very old man meeting a crowd of youngsters, in whose lives and ways he had no part nor interest.

The whale went down to depths where there was so much tiny life in the ocean that the water took its very color from the minute sea crustaceans. With his cavernous mouth wide open, he swam at full speed through the school of little sea creatures. He closed his mouth, and when he lifted his tongue water drained out between the rows of bone-like structure which formed a miniature forest within the whale's head. The myriad of creatures which the whale had taken caught on the hair-like growth with which the baleen, or whale bone, was covered.

The whale swallowed his food, forcing it down a throat so small that a fish as large as a herring would have passed through only with difficulty, and turned to swim back into the school of tiny animals. He fed again and again, until his appetite was satisfied. No longer hungry, the whale lolled for a while in the ocean's depths.

He swerved, turning his colossal body like a great

torpedo, and rose slowly toward the surface. The black water became gray, then light, until finally the sun penetrated it. The whale broke the surface, levelled, and expelled the spent air from his lungs. It shot high into the air, a mist-like spume, and wafted away. The whale drew clean air through his nostrils, two apertures on top of his head. When he continued his journey, he stayed on the surface.

He swam slowly past a herd of walrus that were playing in the water. On the edge of the ice he saw a polar bear that looked curiously at him. But the whale was interested in none of these creatures.

There had been a time when it became sheer joy to follow these sea roads, to be part of a herd of whales whose backs cut the water cleanly as they played and raced. At that time the whale had been young, and filled with life. Now he was old and lonely. He still swam north when the water opened, and south when it closed, because he had been doing it for years and ingrained habit was too powerful to break now.

But there was no longer any zest in exploring the sea lanes, for there were no longer old companions with whom he could swim. Of the great herd which had once travelled with him, all except the old whale had fallen to Eskimo hunters or to other hazards of the sea. Other herds of whales still swam north, but the old whale wanted no part of them.

He travelled for three days, eating as he went. He came to a deep bay which he knew well, and fed on the small life in its depths. He came up to breathe, sounded again, and came up a second time.

His tail stirred and his flukes moved slightly as he watched the things that were bearing down upon him. He was alert, but not frightened. Age and experience had taught him much, and the old whale knew that he could not run away from this danger.

There were six in the herd of orcas, or killer whales, bearing down upon him. No one of the six was a third of the old whale's length or a tenth of his weight, but they were agile, savage things armed with rows of slashing teeth that would attack anything. Like sharks, their appetites were never satisfied; an orca might kill a dozen seals before it stopped hunting.

The six swam abreast, their big back fins cutting the water, and bore down upon the old whale like wolves charging an embattled caribou bull. The whale turned to face them. When they did not swerve, he smashed forward like a sixty-five-foot battering ram.

The orcas anticipated his move, and streamed smoothly past, three on either side. Flanking the old whale, they closed in for the attack. An orca slashed like a wolf at the whale's lips and retreated. Another darted in, and another, each attacking the old whale's vulnerable lips.

The whale sounded, diving deep into the water and swimming as fast as he could go. But he did not flee with the blind terror of a younger animal. This whale was an experienced battler. Like an old wolf-stricken moose, he put his faith in strategy.

Sea wolves that they were, the bloodthirsty orcas streamed after him.

The whale went down and down. He knew this part of the sea as well as he knew all the rest. The pack ice here, because of constant currents and winds, was always in motion. Ice coming in from the sea ground at the pack, and when it could not force a way through it fought its way to the top. Heaped and twisted, this ice was more than a hundred and fifty feet thick, its bottom a maze of caverns and tunnels that varied from a few feet to several dozen yards in width. With the attacking orcas in close pursuit, the whale swam into such a tunnel.

He stopped suddenly. The whale had known, as the orcas had not, that he would find a narrow place in the winding tunnel. But the orcas did not care.

Maddened now by the streams of blood that flowed from the whale, they pushed on relentlessly. They had never yet found anything they feared or anything that would not flee from them. Like smoothly cast spears they glided in to the attack.

The whale thrashed his flukes and flipped his huge tail. In that narrow tunnel he struck an orca every time he moved. Still gripped with blood lust, the killers bore in. But here they could not attack, for there was no room in which to maneuver; the whale's floundering body filled the tunnel. Flung against the ice wall with tremendous force, an orca quivered and turned over, white belly up. Two more, finally seeking escape, were smashed by the whale's tossing tail. The whale struggled still more furiously.

When he finally stopped thrashing, there were no orcas left to attack him. All six had been smashed against the walls of the tunnel. It was as though a bull moose or caribou had maneuvered land wolves into a narrow canyon where they were unable to evade his striking hooves.

The whale swam very slowly through the tunnel and out the other side. The water behind him was red, and blood still streamed from the many savage wounds which the orcas had inflicted. But the old whale felt very little pain. He simply swam slower and slower, until all movement ceased. Only a trickle flowed from his bleeding wounds, and then even that stopped. The old whale had lived a long and good life in the sea. Even in his last battle, he had deported himself as befitted a creature of dignity and stature.

Now at last the sea received him with proper respect. The whale drifted slowly with the current for a long while. It was almost three weeks before a fierce storm snarled across the water, and strong waves finally deposited his body on the arctic shore.

Half a thousand yards up on the shore that stretched away from the Bay of Seals, Kalak lay on her back. All four paws were in the air, and her head drooped lazily to one side as she let the warm sun play over her belly.

Its warmth was pleasant, for the summer sun was sinking every day. Last night, at midnight, it had dipped nearer to the horizon than it had been in months. Open leads in the Bay of Seals were forming a thick scum of ice, and the seals which normally splashed and frolicked in the open leads had to spend more and more time pushing their noses through ice so they could breathe.

Kalak flopped to her side, raised her head, and glanced at the cub, who lay on a sunny slope twenty yards away. The cub was fast asleep, with his head resting on his flank. Kalak rose sleepily, stretched and yawned, and went back to the shore.

Kalak stood still, looking down a slope of smooth ice that ended at an open lead. She saw a seal lying at the edge of the ice. Kalak sniffed, but though she was hungry, she was not yet hungry enough to exert the effort necessary to catch a meal. She bent her head into the stiff north wind, and shuffled her feet uneasily as she read the message the wind brought.

Winter was coming, and when it arrived all the open leads in the Bay of Seals would be covered by three feet of ice. The seals would remain as long as the shrimp swarmed and fish were plentiful, but no polar bear would be able to catch them under the protecting ice. When winter came the best hunting would lie out on the pack, where there were always open leads and seals to use them. Sensing the approach of winter, most of the polar bears which had found summer hunting at the Bay of Seals had already departed for their winter hunting grounds. Only a few, of which Kalak's mate was one, still remained.

Kalak looked again at the basking seal, as the wind brought her mate's scent to her. Kalak sat down and awaited the outcome of her mate's stalk. She saw only the seal, as a brown mass on the ice, but the wind continued to carry to her the exact story of what her mate was doing. Kalak knew when he came near the seal, and when the scent of her mate and that of the seal came to her with equal strength, she knew that he was almost ready to strike. Then Kalak saw her cub.

He appeared on top of the smooth ice that sloped down to the lead, a gangling thing, still possessed of a cub's awkwardness. The cub ran a happy tongue out, and with reckless enthusiasm flung himself down the slope. Sliding on his fat belly, he sailed gaily past the seal and frightened it into the water a second before Kalak's mate could have made his kill.

The big male rose, bellowing his rage, and flung himself into the water where the cub's wild slide had dumped him. Hearing his father's bawls of anger, and trying frantically to escape punishment, the cub swam across the lead, climbed out on the far side, and raced parallel to it. Kalak's mate swam after him.

Kalak ran, quartering on a course that would bring her between the cub and his angry father. She plunged into the lead, swam across, and climbed out to face her mate. He hesitated, then came a step nearer and stopped again when Kalak snarled. The big male's roaring subsided to a few threatening grumbles. He knew the fury of an aroused mother bear, and obviously Kalak was willing to fight if he would not let the cub alone.

The big male turned away and, with an air of decision, started off across the ice. When he came to an open lead he swam straight across, and kept going. Kalak raised her head to watch while the chastened cub came in to crouch at her heels. The big male did not swerve or look back. The last Kalak saw of him, he was far out on the pack and still trekking steadily northward.

Three days later, except for Kalak and her cub, there were no polar bears on the Bay of Seals.

Chapter IV

THE MIST BEAR

Chuesandrin sat on an old sealskin spread on the floor of his tent and reflected upon the various problems in the devil-driver's trade. While he meditated, he chewed on a small piece of meat from the caribou Agtuk had brought down.

Chuesandrin sighed wistfully. It would be a priceless asset for any devil-driver if there really were devils which he could control at will. Then, if the devil-driver did not fancy the treatment he received at the hands of the villagers, he could simply order one of his devils to drive all the game away. As soon as the villagers repented their sins, and made proper atonement, the devil could be instructed to bring the game back.

Unfortunately, he had no devils. That would still not be too serious if Agtuk did not understand the lack of devils as well as Chuesandrin did. But Agtuk did understand. What was worse, he now had half the village believing as he did, instead of having everyone believe in Chuesandrin. If enough people swung about to Agtuk's viewpoint it was even possible that he, Chuesandrin, would have to get out and hunt for a living, instead of demanding and receiving tribute from those who did hunt. That in itself would be intolerable enough. But Chuesandrin had an even more difficult and immediate problem to solve.

He didn't like Natkus, Agtuk's dog, and so he had put a devil in the dog. Chuesandrin had sincerely believed, when he bade the devil go live in Natkus, that the pressure of public opinion would bring Agtuk to kill his favorite hunting dog. Apparently Agtuk not only cared nothing for public opinion, but he had even dared tell the devil-driver that he, personally, would be held responsible for Natkus' safety.

Chuesandrin sighed again. He knew perfectly well that there wasn't any game and that there was little likelihood of any. However, after he had had his revenge on Natkus, he had planned to create a special omen that would tell the villagers that they had best move to other hunting grounds. Now Agtuk had forestalled him even there. He had said it first.

That placed Chuesandrin in a bad dilemma. He knew as well as Agtuk that the hunters would find good hunting in the Bay of Seals. After they found it, and remembered that the devil-driver had prophesied that they would find only devils, the whole village might doubt Chuesandrin. And that, from a devil-driver's viewpoint, would be disastrous.

Chuesandrin made his decision. He would take the devil out of Natkus.

He rose, rummaged in a miscellaneous pile of odds and ends until he found what he sought, and looked critically at it. Actually, it was a spool of ordinary black thread, but to Chuesandrin it was the tiniest and most fragile thing he had ever seen. Obviously the Eskimo who had traded it to Chuesandrin for half a walrus tusk had wandered too long in the sun. He claimed that he had received the thread from strange men with white skin and beards on their faces. They talked an unknown gibberish, the Eskimo had said, and travelled in an oomiak larger than the biggest whale. Chuesandrin had listened gravely to the silly tale because he had not wished to discourage the trade. Though the thread had no practical use, he had thought that it might some time be well adapted to devil-driving. That time was here.

Chuesandrin sliced another chunk from his share of the caribou which Agtuk had killed and held it in his hand. Then he cut the chunk in two and put half of it back. Devils could be tempted with very little and, on the whole, devil-drivers probably had the healthier appetite. Chuesandrin snapped off ten feet of thread, tied one end to the meat, coiled the thread carefully, and put both that and the meat in a sleeve of his caribou-skin jacket.

When he walked out of his tent he looked neither to the right nor the left, but only ahead. He bent to pick up a few willow sticks, scraped tinder from them, and caught up two chunks of iron pyrite that were lying beside the sticks. Then he looked up and suddenly stiffened.

The tents of those hunters who were going to the Bay of Seals buzzed with activity, and the tents of those who must help move the village were only a little less active. Nobody except a few children had had time to glance up at the crest of a near-by hill and see a herd of caribou winding around it, and the children were too busy staring at the devil-driver to pay attention to anything else.

Chuesandrin knelt down, arranged his tinder and sticks, struck a spark into the tinder, and blew it until a flame arose. With grave deliberation he arranged his meat on the ground, roared at the children until they fled, uncoiled the thread, and, except for enough to reach from his hand to the ground, covered it with dust. Then he called Agtuk imperatively.

The hunter came to the door of his lodge, saw who had summoned him, and turned to go back in. Chuesandrin raised his voice.

"I have found a way to drive the devil out of Natkus, and thus to insure hunting success in the Bay of Seals! Would you dare risk failure when success can certainly be had?"

Attracted by the devil-driver's shouting, other hunters gathered about. Their women hung in the background, looking alternately at Chuesandrin and at Agtuk. Their faces were questioning, tense. Agtuk hesitated. He didn't believe in devils, but some of his people never would lose their fear of them. They would go to the Bay of Seals anyway, but they would go happier and be more eager if they thought there were no devils to mar their prospects.

"Speak to the point and swiftly, devil-driver. I have hunting equipment to make ready."

"Bring Natkus," Chuesandrin directed. Then remembering that Natkus had chased him across the village, he added, "but hold him."

Agtuk approached, his hand resting lightly on Natkus' head.

"Let the dog come near the meat," Chuesandrin directed, "but not near enough to seize it. I think that the devil will jump out of Natkus into the meat when he smells it. If so, all of you will see the meat move when the devil enters it."

The villagers waited tensely. Agtuk wrapped his hand in Natkus' hair, and let him approach the meat. Natkus strained forward. When his nose was almost touching the chunk of caribou, Chuesandrin jerked his thread.

"Ai!" he shrieked, rushing forward. "The devil entered the meat! All of you saw it move!"

Chuesandrin scooped up meat and thread, ran to the fire, and threw both in.

"The devil is burned!" he chortled. "Now there can be no doubt of wonderful hunting at the Bay of Seals!"

The devil-driver passed his hand over the fire and the flame burned red.

"A sign!" he shrieked. "A good sign! There will be food for all while we are moving to the Bay of Seals! If hunters will go there—" he pointed toward the valley into which he had seen the caribou disappear —"there will be meat in plenty! Approach carefully and shoot well, for there will be many caribou! I, Chuesandrin, say this."

Later that evening Agtuk entered Chuesandrin's tent. In one hand he held a choice caribou head, while in the other he bore something else.

"Here," he grinned, extending the head. "Meat for a devil-driver from a hunter. And here—" Agtuk extended his other hand, about which was wound the remnants of the black thread—"is your devil, Chuesandrin, the very one that made the meat move when Natkus' devil entered it." He smiled. "It makes no difference even if you are a rogue. The village is happy again and the hunters are eager! There will be good times ahead!"

After the hunters had secured so much caribou meat that no person or dog in the village was in any immediate danger of hunger, they were in no hurry to start for the Bay of Seals. There were harpoons and lances to be sharpened, and new weapons to be made. Knives, bows and arrows, and thongs had to be checked in order to insure that they would not fail when they were most needed. The oomiak in which Agtuk and his seven companions, as well as their dogs and gear, would precede the village, must be examined and repaired very carefully. When they were well on their journey, there would be neither time nor adequate facilities for such repair work. Meanwhile, as long as there was plenty of meat, why pine for more? Nobody was hungry.

Throughout, Agtuk fretted. His lances and harpoons, as well as his bows and arrows, were always in such good repair that he could snatch up any weapon in his lodge and, at a moment's notice, be ready for the hunt. He always knew the quality of his clothing and dog harness and, when that quality became impaired in any way, Larensa repaired it. He lived by hunting, therefore he must always be ready to hunt.

Every day, while the village feasted or, under the pretense of preparing for the journey, idled, he journeyed into the hills to seek more caribou or out on the ice to look for seals. Twice he found, stalked, and harpooned seals. There was nothing else; the caribou had not returned to the haunts in which they were usually found nor had many seals come back to the leads. So Agtuk worried, while the village consumed the plenty it had discovered in one providential herd of caribou.

Instead of remaining high for twenty-four hours, and little different at night than it was at noon, the sun had started its dip below the horizon when Toolah approached him.

"All is ready for the start," he announced. "My harpoons and lances are sharp, my fishing gear is in order, my best dog is fat and eager to go."

"And," Agtuk said dryly, "there is little food remaining in your wife's cooking pot."

Toolah nodded gravely. "It is true that we should have started for the Bay of Seals when we had much food to see us through."

"Are the others as ready as you?" Agtuk asked.

"They are. Chuesandrin has also prepared a charm for each of us in order that we may be safe on our journey. Here is yours, Agtuk."

"Chuesandrin also sees a shortage of food soon," Agtuk observed as he tucked the bit of twisted grass inside his shirt. "Very well, Toolah. We start tomorrow, as soon as the sun is high enough to melt the ice that will form when it sinks tonight. Tell the others to be ready."

Natkus came to greet him when Agtuk went to his own lodge. He petted the dog briefly, sank down on his skin-covered couch, and almost instantly was fast asleep. His was the rest of a hunter, who may have to remain awake for hours without end, and who can sleep for many hours when an opportunity presents.

Agtuk rose when the sun was again high. He ate heartily of the boiled caribou and seal blubber which Larensa had cooked for him, gathered up his selected hunting weapons, and strode down to the sea where the oomiak waited.

Now an eager longing to be away possessed him. He was Agtuk, the hunter. The strongest and most skillful of the Endorah, he was responsible for all. He knew that, at last, all were setting out to a place of plenty. It was a good place, one where the old people, the children, the hunters, and even the dogs, could find so much food that they might eat until they could hold no more. With ill-concealed impatience Agtuk awaited the coming of the seven who were to go with him.

Each man came accompanied by his favorite dog and carrying his best weapons, as well as that portion of food which he had allotted to see him through the journey. Agtuk helped with the loading of the sledge which was meant to carry the oomiak over ice fields where no open water existed. Then he said goodbye to Larensa.

"Be of good cheer," he bade her. "Give no heed to Chuesandrin, who will try to take everything over, now that I am gone, and watch yourself on the journey. Depend on no one else."

"I will remember, Agtuk," she smiled.

He caught up a paddle and did not glance back as the oomiak slid down a long open lead. The eager restlessness grew within him. Was he not Agtuk, strong man of the Ice People? Being strong, he had strength to give to others; this was the way his tribe must always go. When no game lived near them, they had to move to the game. It had always been so and it always would be so. Neither devil-drivers, nor great storms, nor intense cold, nor anything else, would ever change that.

When they came to the ice at the end of the lead they climbed out, lifted the oomiak, and placed it upon the sled they had brought for the purpose. The eight dogs were harnessed and hitched to the sled. Agtuk led the way across the apparently trackless ice fields, while the dogs strained behind him and his seven companions walked beside the dogs. Agtuk watched the ice, the sun, and the way the snow drifts slanted. By such signs he guided himself and those who came with him.

When they were tired they set their skin tent up on the pack ice, tied the dogs, poured a little seal oil into a cooking lamp, boiled caribou meat, and ate. When they had rested they were off again. Late that day, scouting ahead of the rest, Agtuk found and killed a seal. They did not linger here, because the dogs, marching steadily over the ice, gave no sign that there were other seals. Thus, eating when they were hungry and resting when they were tired, travelling in the oomiak where there was open water and over the ice where there was none, on the seventh day they came to the Bay of Seals.

Agtuk looked at it. From repeated freezings, leads which had been open were now ice-locked. Within a few days the ice on those old leads would be strong enough to support a man, but now it was not. However, there was plenty of other ice upon which a man could walk. Agtuk unfastened Natkus and threw the harness in the oomiak.

"Go up on the shore and make camp," he directed

three of the hunters who had accompanied him. "The rest will hunt seals."

Natkus ranged ahead when the hunters walked on the ice. Presently, he stopped to snuffle in the snow. Careful not to jar the ice or make any noise, one of the hunters walked to the dog's side, brushed some of the snow away, and probed with the end of his spear until he had found a seal's breathing hole. He thrust a slim ivory bobber into the hole and stood with his spear poised.

Agtuk called Natkus, and the four remaining hunters walked over the ice until the dog found another breathing hole. They left a hunter there and searched out three more holes. Agtuk stayed at the last one, and bade Natkus lie down at his side.

He waited, his spear ready, unwavering eyes fixed on the slender ivory bobber that thrust above the snow. This sort of hunting called for endless patience as well as absolute silence, for any seal might have a dozen breathing holes and it could be hours before he came to a hole where a hunter waited. If there was the least alien sound the seal would not come at all.

However, this time Agtuk had stood for scarcely five minutes when, pushed sharply by something beneath the ice, the ivory bobber came up through the hole. Agtuk thrust hard with his spear, and felt it go through the ice deep into a seal. The hunter gripped his spear with both hands, and grinned broadly. When he looked about, his grin widened. Of the five hunters who had poised beside breathing holes, two besides himself had already thrust their spears and found game.

The hunters who had gone to set up camp came running with axes and ice chisels, and chopped the seals out of the ice. Agtuk looked at Nalee and Moostantin, the two others who had struck game.

"Is this not rightly called the Bay of Seals?" he asked.

"Aye," Moostantin agreed happily. "Thanks to the wisdom and foresight of Agtuk, we shall winter amid plenty!"

That day the hunters took nine seals, and more on each succeeding day, until, when the rest of the village arrived, there was enough seal meat, blubber and oil, to assure them of food and fuel for many weeks to come.

The day after the village was set up, Moostantin took two dogs and set off across the ice on an exploring trip. Less than an hour after he had left the village, he staggered painfully back. Half his parka and fawn-skin undershirt were torn away. Blood streamed down his arm.

Agtuk ran to meet him and Toolah caught him as he fell. Agtuk bent over him.

"What did you see?" he asked. "What did you meet out on the ice?"

Moostantin raised his head. "Kalak," he whispered.

"The mist bear!" Toolah exclaimed.

"The mist bear," Moostantin agreed weakly. "The great bear that no one except me has ever met. It was Kalak, for there are no other bears like her. She came with her cub, which I wounded with my spear. Then Kalak attacked me, and would have killed me had not my dogs interfered." Moostantin smiled wanly. "Now I may be almost as great a hunter as you, Agtuk, for I have fought with Kalak."

Larensa and Moostantin's wife helped the wound-ed hunter into his lodge. Agtuk raced to his tent. Whenever hunters had gathered and talked among themselves, many had been the tales of Kalak, the bear that could change into mist. Although Kalak's tracks were always recognized, she herself was never seen. Now she was here, within striking distance of the camp, and had already wounded a hunter. However, Agtuk thought grimly, she also had a wounded cub with her.

Agtuk snatched up his sharpest lance, called Natkus to his side, and joined the nine hunters who were already plunging down onto the ice. The dog pack ran with them as they followed the trail Moostantin had made. They found Moostantin's two dogs, already stiffly frozen.

The great bear track and the smaller cub's track leading away from the bodies of the two dogs were plain. The pack snarled happily away.

Kalak stayed on the Bay of Seals long after the rest of the polar bears were gone. Only after the ice became too thick to smash with her paw and open a way to the seals beneath it, did she start to guide her cub back toward the easier hunting in the center of the ice pack.

She was fat and the cub had grown, for all summer long they had had rich hunting. Also, throughout the season, they had encountered no human beings. The absence of people, the only creatures she feared, had made the giant bear more careless than she had ever been. She was confident of her ability to protect the cub.

Kalak quartered along the shore, taking the easiest route to the hunting grounds she wanted to reach. Since the wind was blowing hard from her toward the camp, she did not smell the Eskimo village until she was within a mile of it.

She stopped, swinging her head about as she sought more evidence of the human beings who had again encroached upon her hunting grounds. The cub paced ahead and disappeared among some ice hummocks. Again Kalak caught the elusive scent that had startled her.

Then, so near that its full warmth was carried into her nostrils, she got the scent of Moostantin and his two dogs. Down among ice hummocks, Moostantin had been below the level of the wind that swept over them. Now, scarcely two hundred yards away, he climbed over the ridge of an ice hummock and his scent became very plain. At the same time Kalak heard the two dogs yell. Her cub bawled in pain.

Swiftly as only a polar bear can, Kalak ran over the uneven ice. At all times, because of the cub, she had tried to avoid human beings. Now Kalak's fear evaporated. Half a ton of blazing fury, she hurled herself toward the thing that had dared hurt her cub. She would have charged a whole village full of Eskimos.

She burst around a hummock and saw the cub. Blood bubbled out of the wound in his shoulder where Moostantin had thrust with his lance, and stained his white fur. The cub had backed against an ice hummock where, with snarling lips, he faced the two hysterical dogs that beset him. Moostantin, trying for a new thrust with his lance, did not hear Kalak come.

The big ice bear charged recklessly, intent upon the most immediate threat to her cub. She paused only a second as she passed Moostantin, struck his shoulder a glancing blow, and sent him spinning across the ice. Kalak pounced upon the two dogs, grasped one in her grinding jaws, and slapped the other with her right paw. The dogs died so swiftly that they were scarcely aware of the fury that struck them down. Agile as a cat, Kalak turned toward the man.

He had risen, she saw, and was staggering over the ice. Kalak took half a dozen furious strides toward him but, when the cub whimpered, she turned back.

The cub moved out from his ice hummock, snuffled at the two dogs, and struck them a furious blow with his unwounded paw. He growled, and limped painfully toward Kalak. The mother bear examined him anxiously.

Though Moostantin's lance had thrust falsely, and

missed the heart, it had gone deep. The cub curled his right paw beneath him, and red streaked the ice over which he moved. Kalak gently licked his wound with her warm tongue. A sudden desperation rose within her. For two years she had revolved her life around this cub and devoted all her attention to seeing him grow up. Now she saw that he was badly wounded.

She fully realized the peril of the situation. She already knew that there was an Eskimo camp not far away. If one hunter was prowling the ice there might be more. Kalak bent her head very close to her cub, as though questioning him, then turned and started at right angles to the direction she had been taking. The cub limped behind her.

Kalak turned her head, her anxiety growing. She would like to travel fast, but the cub's best pace was an awkward gallop. Kalak slowed her own pace sufficiently to let the cub stay beside her. Then she let him lead and dropped behind. If danger came, it would approach from the rear.

They journeyed straight out across the Bay, toward the depths of the pack ice. Faintly behind them Kalak thought she heard the yelling of dogs, and deliberately dropped farther behind the straining cub. Regardless of what happened to her, the cub must get away.

The cub tried to climb an ice hummock, fell down, picked himself up, and started again. This time he got over the top and slid down the other side. The cold and the wind had healed the cub's wound so that it did not bleed any more, but he was still unable to use his right front paw, and could not travel as fast as Kalak would have liked to go.

The mother bear climbed the hummock, and for a moment stood on top of it, the better to scan her back trail. She saw nothing, but now she was certain that she heard dogs yelling in the distance. Kalak followed her cub down the hummock and into the humped ice field on the other side. The desperate fear within her was now allayed by hope.

There was a chance of escaping and she knew it, for from ahead came the distinct scent of open water. If they could reach that ahead of the hunters, and swim across, their pursuers might not be able to follow. The cub tried hard to scrape his way up another hummock, but fell back again. Kalak ran past, round the end of the slope. If the cub was unable to climb she would have to choose an easier path for him. The smell of open water became more pronounced.

Then Kalak saw the lead, a great expanse of water

with jagged ice peninsulas jutting into it. So far away that it was only vaguely distinguishable, she saw the pack ice on the other side. Behind, the yelling of the pack was very plain. The dogs were almost upon them.

Kalak came to the edge of the ice and without hesitation leaped in. She turned, making a rippling swirl in the water as she tried to coax the cub in. Instead of leaping in behind her, he stopped on the edge of the ice, his wounded paw curled beside him. The cub knew what Kalak did not—he could no longer swim.

A confused brown and gray mass against the ice's white background, the dogs swept into sight and set up a great yelping. Kalak climbed back out on the ice and led the cub out onto one of the ice peninsulas. Then she swung at bay, facing the pack.

The pack raced up to her, stopped just short of striking distance, and increased their racket. With the unerring eye of a trained fighter, Kalak selected Natkus from the rest of the pack. He was the biggest and most dangerous.

She leaped like a cat at Natkus, but when she struck he was no longer there. Kalak swung her great hooked claws at another dog, and swept it off the ice into the water. Then the pack closed in, biting at her flanks

and rear. Kalak brushed them off, and retreated to
stand before her cub. A great snarl rippled from her
throat when she saw Agtuk lead the hunters into sight.
She could charge the hunters but if she did the cub
would be at the mercy of the dogs. She must stay
where she could defend him.

Bolder now, with the arrival of their masters, the
pack surged in again. The cub dragged himself painfully to Kalak's side, and faced the pack with snarling
jaws. Cub though he was, he was still a polar bear,
ready to fight.

Kalak swung her ponderous head toward Agtuk.
She sensed that just as Natkus excelled among the
dogs, so did this hunter among the men.

The men began to close in on her. She bit at Nalee's
lance, splintered it in her jaws, and then whirled
furiously at a hunter who was creeping up on the cub.
Before she could strike, the hunter's lance flicked
forward and the cub sprawled flat on the ice. Kalak
bounded forward, caught the man who had killed
her cub, and crushed his head with one sledge-hammer blow.

She felt Agtuk's lance burn into her side, then
another and another. She lunged forward, roaring
defiance, but now she could no longer see clearly

either the men or the dogs. She was only dimly aware
of figures, and turned this way and that, striking
blindly.

Then she heard a splintering crash and saw the
figures leap wildly to regain the safety of the pack ice.
The long arm that jutted into the open lead had
broken off. Carrying the wounded Kalak with it, the
ice cake floated out to sea.

Chapter V

BLOOD ON THE ICE

Wind lashed out of the northeast, swooped low to the water, and blew it into rolling waves that tossed the ice cake high and let it fall. A gull came out of the sky to hover above the wounded bear. Another gull joined it, and then another. They did not move their wings, but dipped and whirled or rose and fell according to the wind currents. As they circled and dipped, the gulls squawked in indecision.

A hundred times had each gull feasted on seals killed by polar bears or caribou killed by wolves. They were experienced scavengers whose business it was to clean up refuse left on the ice, and they knew just how to go about it. But now they hesitated. There was a polar bear beneath them and even though it looked dead, it still commanded fear and respect. The gulls swooped lower, and still lower, until finally their courage had risen to the point where the boldest among them dared to light on the ice cake. It stood with wings poised, ready to take to the air again at a second's notice. The gull bent its head to look at Kalak.

Though the gull had come down to previous bears when they killed game, it had not been afraid. Those bears had been busy with the seals they had killed and, as soon as they finished eating, they went their way and left the rest to the gulls. But this bear had no seal. There was something unusual about it, something foreign to the gull's experience with bears. Was Kalak merely resting on the ice or was she, as the gull hoped, dead? The gull uttered a tentative squawk, and when Kalak did not move the gull squawked again. Its two companions came hastily down.

For a moment they stood on the edge of the ice, as far from Kalak as they could get. Suddenly they rose, flapping their wings as they ascended three or four feet into the air. They hovered directly over the motionless bear. Certainly she was dead.

In the depths of the sea over which the ice cake

floated, a shadow moved. It rose from the depths into translucent water, and the clear outline of a single orca was framed in the sea. Coming farther up, the orca broke water with its great back fin. It swam clear around the ice, then charged full speed toward it. The orca rammed the ice cake with its head, hoping to tip it so that Kalak would slide into the water. But the killer whale succeeded only in bringing consciousness back to the hurt bear.

When Kalak raised her head, the gulls screamed away and disappeared. With a great effort the bear rose, tearing out quantities of fur that had frozen in the blood which had bubbled from her onto the ice. She was no longer bleeding; the cold had stopped her wound. Kalak staggered two weak steps and sank to a sitting position. She whimpered plaintively and looked about for the cub. He was not with her. Kalak swung slowly about to face the direction from which the ice cake had drifted.

She remembered now, and memory of the thing that had been done to her brought a consuming rage. She took a weak step forward, but fell and lay where she had fallen. Reaching forward with her front paws, she tried to hook them into the ice and pull herself on. The cake of ice had drifted so far that she could not

even see the pack from which it had broken, but she still wished to swim back and renew the battle with the Eskimos.

Coming in with smashing force, the orca struck the floating ice again. A long sliver broke away and fell into the sea, and the ice split a few inches from the place where Kalak lay.

She looked over the edge of the ice and saw the orca, which now lay motionless in the water, looking up at her. Kalak tried to raise a paw to strike at it. She knew orcas, and what they could do, but she was not afraid of them. She dragged herself nearer to the edge of the ice. The orca rose, slashed, missed, and fell back. Kalak tried again to raise her paw and strike, but could not. She had lost too much blood.

The orca smashed the ice cake again and again. Failing to break or tip it, the killer followed along on top of the water, hungry eyes fixed on Kalak. When she struggled again to her feet, stumbled, and almost slid into the water, the orca darted eagerly forward, only to be disappointed again. Kalak had crawled farther up on the ice. The orca continued to follow the ice raft.

The sun had fallen behind the horizon, and twilight had taken the place of constant daylight, when the friendly wind at last shoved the ice cake against the pack's solid barrier. The eager orca waited just off the edge of the solid ice, hoping the bumping of the ice cake would dislodge the bear.

Then a tremendous wave rolled in and heaved the cake clear up on the solid pack.

Kalak rose, and stood for an unsteady moment. She fell from the ice cake and picked herself up. Slowly, her head bent and her black nose almost brushing the ice, she walked farther up on the pack. It was a shambling walk, for weakness was again creeping over her. With an effort she raised her head, and stared at the pale stars that had bloomed in the sky. She knew she should eat, but she could not hunt.

A white shadow flitted by, and one of the tiny arctic foxes emerged from a hummock to stare for a moment at her. The fox slipped silently back.

Kalak fought slowly on, threading her way around hummocks that she could no longer go over. She paused a moment, as though listening for something that should be on her back trail, and continued.

A mile from where her cake of ice had bumped the barrier, she came to a high knoll. Kalak stopped, and raised her head while she studied it. Like a small hill, the knoll was merely a heap of ice on the ice pack. It had been higher, but the summer sun had melted its peaked top down to a flat one. Melting ice water, running down the side of the knoll, had worn a sloping gully.

Kalak climbed the gully. Ordinarily she would have ascended it easily, but now she had to labor up the slope. She was breathless and almost without strength when she reached the summit. She walked out on the flat top and looked all about, satisfied that it was the safest place she could find in her weakened condition. Then she lay down to rest.

Kalak lay quietly on her icy retreat while the sun rose, set, and rose again. She was patient, accepting this period as only a wild creature would accept it. Events to come must take one of two courses; she would die here or she would recover and leave. Even while death hovered near she fought it because she did not know how to do anything else. Her entire life had been a battle for things which she must have, and the smallest fiber within her had never surrendered to anything.

After she had lain for more than thirty hours on top of the knoll, the natural strength and resiliency of her tough body asserted themselves. She was still weak, and the natural senses with which she was endowed told her that it would be best not to move too much until she could do so freely. But she was definitely better.

She stood up, looked about the top of the knoll, and moved to the gully up which she had climbed. Anything else that came would try to ascend the same way; it was a good defensive position.

It was there that Kalak met the wolves.

For five days the wolf pack had ranged the frozen wastes without finding game weak enough or unprotected enough to be pulled down. In the hope of surprising an unwary seal, they had swung back to the edge of the ice barrier. Coursing along the open water, they came to Kalak's abandoned ice raft.

Ordinarily, the wolves would have followed the bear's tracks cautiously, hoping for no more than the frozen remains of her kills. But the scent of blood showed that this bear was wounded. Moreover, the wolves were desperate with hunger. The pack swung about on Kalak's trail, red tongues lolling, fangs gleaming in their murderous open mouths.

They came leaping across the ice, crying and eager, positive that the trail they were on would lead them to a wounded and helpless beast. A big white wolf led by ten lengths, and flung himself recklessly up the gully.

The pack followed, the animals in the rear trying to push ahead.

Far-off, suddenly cracking ice muffled the white leader's shrill cry as Kalak struck him. He went down with the first blow, his back broken. Kalak's weakness was overcome by flaming anger. Long ago, this same pack of wolves had come to another far-off place. Kalak had not been present when they came, but her two tiny cubs had been, and she never saw them again. The enraged ice bear struck again, and again. She even slid down the gully, eager to get into the thickest of the fight. With no room in which to dodge the bear's murderous claws, and pushed on by those behind, each wolf had to meet the enraged Kalak alone.

When she was finished, only one wolf raced back across the ice in the direction from which it had come. Kalak reared on her hind legs, growling, then dropped back on the ice. She pulled a dead wolf to her and began to eat.

Five days later she left the knoll and shuffled off across the ice. She was not hungry for she had fed on the wolves, but she was very thin. Her skin sagged in heavy folds, and for the first time she felt the wind that keened across the ice pack.

Now she must have food, not lean wolf but the rich fat and blubber to which she was accustomed. Kalak sat down to rest, then went on. She stalked and missed a seal beside an open lead. A second time she failed to strike game. She shambled on, still sick and weak.

Then she caught a rich and heavy odor that blew from the arctic shore. Kalak swung her head, turned at an angle to the course she had been following, and pursued the enticing scent. It was the dead whale.

Kalak strode steadily forward, not swerving or hesitating even though, with the scent of the whale, came the odors of other animals which had already found it. She could smell another polar bear, one of those from the Bay of Seals, and many of the little white foxes. There was also the faint odor of wolves. Kalak walked faster. She hated all wolves, and if she could lure another pack into battle she would do so.

But of prime importance now was plenty of rich food to renew her wasted strength; she could do little else until she had eaten that food. The sun went down, and the stars came out before Kalak saw the whale.

The first waves had brought it gently to the beach, but succeeding angry seas had carried it farther up until it was entirely clear of the water. A long, high mass that looked almost black in the pale light cast by the flickering stars, the whale lay with its great head upon the beach and its tail toward the sea.

Only slightly larger than a big cat, a small fox frisked down to the ice to meet Kalak when she came. Not yet completely white, the fox's fur was fast acquiring that snowy shade which it would have when the sun rose not at all and twenty-four hours of darkness closed over the arctic sea. Unhurriedly he moved a little to one side when Kalak passed him, and sat down again, curling his bushy tail about his front paws and lifting first one paw and then the other.

Kalak glanced disinterestedly at him and continued. In summer she shared her kills with the ubiquitous gulls, but most of them had already departed for the south and open water. Now the little foxes, which had spent the whole summer back from the sea rearing their families, and living on hares, lemmings, birds, and birds' eggs while they did so, had returned to the shore. When winter arrived one or more foxes would attach themselves to each polar bear and follow it all the time, knowing that they could live luxuriously on whatever the big ice bears discarded.

Kalak was aware that, when she passed, the little fox fell obediently in behind her, but gave no more thought to her follower. For as long as she could remember, when she had been on the ice in winter, one or more foxes were her constant companions. She did not mind because the foxes were mild and inoffensive little creatures. They never interfered with her and certainly were incapable of doing her harm. The foxes wanted only such food as she could not eat.

Having already gorged himself on the dead whale, the fox sat down a few feet away and curled his tail across his front legs as Kalak went in to eat. The other polar bear which had found the whale, a much smaller female, moved to the other side and continued eating from that safe place. Kalak ignored her. A dozen times during their sojourn at the Bay of Seals she had come across the smaller bear and warned her to get out of the way. The small female had always been careful to avoid Kalak, as she avoided her now.

Kalak bit through the whale's leathery skin and deep into the rich layer of blubber that lay just beneath it. It was cold and partly frozen, but it was rich and good. She ate, spurning the skin and all lean meat and taking only blubber. until her belly could hold no more. Then she lay down for a nap.

But even while she slept her unsleeping nose kept her informed of everything that went on about her. From twenty to thirty of the little foxes ripped and pulled at the dead whale. Occasionally some of them glided away like shadows into the starlit night, but they came back or others came to take their places. Kalak was aware when the other polar bear got up to resume eating. She even knew of the lemmings, the little arctic mice, that moved furtively beneath the dead whale and ate their tiny portions.

Then another scent crossed her nostrils and she came swiftly awake. The little fox which had attached himself to her came in nearer. The other foxes stood still, listening in the darkness and awaiting what would happen. On the other side of the whale, the small polar bear went unconcernedly on with her eating. She had no feud with wolves.

Kalak had, and when the pack she had scented came nearer, she snarled out to meet them. The little foxes moved in behind her. Ordinarily, when a wolf pack came, they fled at the first scent. Now that they had an able champion there was no reason to flee.

Kalak met the wolves in the darkness. Lean, white beasts, scarcely seen against the snow upon which they ran, they appeared almost magically, as though they had somehow risen out of the snow. Now they stopped, stood silently for a moment, and melted back in the direction from which they had come. They had no wish to try conclusions with a polar bear who so obviously wanted to fight with them.

Kalak returned to the dead whale and again filled her belly with blubber. Without resentment she saw the little foxes eat, and the other bear. There was enough meat on the whale to feed them all throughout the winter, if need be. Everything that came, excepting wolves and men, could have a share as far as she was concerned.

The sun rose, climbing into the sky and shining down on the ice pack. But summer warmth did not come with it, and within half an hour even the sun was hidden by thick cloud banks. A few hours afterward twilight had fallen. There were no melted pools or lakes on the ice pack now. The season was advancing swiftly to the twenty-four-hour night.

Kalak saw the little fox which had attached itself to her curl up companionably and watch while she ate. Even when Kalak slept the little fox was seldom more than twenty feet away. He knew as well as Kalak that he might stay at the whale and have plenty to eat all winter, but he didn't want to. Strong within the fox's memory were better and fresher foods which he had eaten and which he would like to eat again, and he could afford to wait. Kalak would not stay forever at this dead whale, and when she left the little fox would go with her.

The next day the smaller female left and a big male polar bear ambled in from the sea—an old, surly brute whose teeth were worn down to stubs. He slapped irritably at the foxes around the whale carcass. They only slid nimbly out of his way. The old bear was too old to move swiftly, and polar bears could not catch foxes anyway. The old bear stayed as far as possible from Kalak. An ill-natured, lonely thing whose usefulness was done, he would have starved to death on the ice had he not found the whale. Never again would he be able to hunt.

As the days passed, the loose folds in Kalak's shaggy skin filled out and tightened. She restored her layer of fat, and her strength. With recovery came restlessness.

One morning, with the gentle little fox so close to her heels that he seemed a cub following its mother, she strode straight away from the whale and out on the ice. Behind them, the foxes and the polar bear who remained about the whale stared solemnly at this foolish pair who would leave an assured meal to take their chances on the ice pack.

Uncaring, Kalak padded swiftly over the frozen

sea, turning her head full into the cold blast that roared across it. She was strong again, she was the old
Kalak who went where she willed because she wanted
it so. There was nothing to stop her and nothing had
better try.

The little white fox trotted contentedly behind. He
knew that he would have plenty to eat if he stayed beside the dead whale, but he had elected to cast his lot
with Kalak, in hope of fresher food. He would hold to
that decision.

Hours later, Kalak stopped to snuffle at the ice; she
smelled a breathing hole where a seal came up for air.
Restlessly she paced about, looking for a way to penetrate the ice and find that seal. But the ice was thick
and the leads frozen.

She nosed around another breathing hole, then
went on. The first sharp hunger in days pinched her
belly. She growled belligerently. Usually the sea ice
was never so thick and strong, or so solidly frozen,
that she was unable to break it. Now it was. The seals
she could smell were as safe as they would have been
encased in steel armor plate.

Lighted by stars, and occasionally by the aurora,
the ice was a nightmarish place of weird shapes and
shadows. There were seals beneath it, for Kalak could

smell them, but excepting for herself and the fox the surface of the ice pack was a vast desert from which all life had fled. And all the while the north wind blew steadily across the pack, cold and pitiless.

The day did not pass. Rather, it blended into a deeper and thicker gloom, an undulating, velvet-like blackness broken by the cold light of the stars. The arctic seemed a frozen void. Kalak and the fox paced steadily through the night, two living specks on a plain of infinite emptiness. As living things, the continuance of their lives depended on their ability to eat other living things. But except for themselves and the seals under the ice, there was no life here in the vast frozen reaches. Where could they find food?

Kalak suddenly thought of the fox in a new light.

Without breaking stride she whirled about and cast herself backward. Invariably the little fox followed her on the left and about ten feet behind. When Kalak lunged she brought both paws down on the fox's accustomed place.

But the fox was not there. There had been no time to think of the bear's lightning-swift pass, but inborn senses inherited from a thousand generations were razor-keen. A split second before the bear's flashing paws cracked down on the ice, he had rolled sideways. Now, with his bushy tail curled about his legs, he sat twenty feet away. He lifted a front paw, held it against his body a second, and put it down on the ice. Then he warmed his other front paw. He knew that Kalak would have killed and eaten him. But that inspired neither fear nor resentment, because the fox understood such actions. He himself, if he were able, would gladly kill and eat anything. The spur of hunger was an old, well-understood feeling.

The little fox barked, softly and appeasingly, and watched the bear with calculating eyes. Again, in turn, he pressed each front paw against his breast. He was ready to spring from another charge should one come. But none did.

As though it were irresistibly attracted by some magnet set in the north, Kalak's head swung in that direction, nostrils flaring. She turned her body, every muscle tense as she probed for more of the faint story she had scented. It came again, the distinct odor of a seal, mingled with that of open water!

When Kalak went forward she advanced slowly, searching with her nose much as a hunting hound does. She padded erratically back and forth until she had found every one of the five breathing holes which this seal had gnawed through the ice. The seal had started his holes when the first thin ice formed, and since then had spent much of his time gnawing. Now, under the thickened ice, the holes were cigar-shaped burrows into which the seal could fit his entire body. At the top, under snow, were small holes through which he drew fresh air. Always, when he returned from the depths where he chased and caught fish or shrimp, the seal had to come to one hole or another and breathe. Whenever they froze over, he had to gnaw them open again.

Having found the seal's breathing holes, Kalak started toward the water which she could smell not far away. She soon reached it, a twenty-foot-wide by two-hundred-foot-long opening just recently parted in the pack. Kalak stood on the edge of the lead, studying it with her eyes and nose as she sought every fact pertinent to her problem. She had been born in the world of ice, and had drawn in her ancestors' accumulated knowledge with her mother's milk. When she finished her investigation she knew that this lead would remain open for some time.

She dived cleanly, going deep into the water and swimming strongly beneath the ice. Hers was a master plan, and one which only a master hunter would dare undertake. If she had made one miscalculation, or now made one error, she would drown under the ice.

She swam straight to an air pocket, came up in it to breathe, then dropped back into the murky depths and looked around.

Ahead of her she saw the seal she was trying to catch. She swam slowly and carefully, anxious not to frighten the animal. She saw the seal drop a fish it had caught and speed away.

The top of the ice pack was dark, but the water had a translucent quality strangely at variance with the night outside. Kalak could see the seal, a dim shape in the distance, glide toward another breathing hole.

With a rush she was away to intercept it. The seal swerved, retreated into water where Kalak could no longer see him, and lurked there. Kalak waited quietly, knowing that he would come back. He had to reach a breathing hole.

When the seal came back he was swimming furiously. A master of the water, more agile and swift than the fish in its depths, he could easily out-swim the bear. But he could not remain away from his breathing holes. Kalak was there to meet him when he swam toward the air which he so desperately needed.

The seal turned to dash away, but could no longer swim fast. The air in his lungs was spent, and his

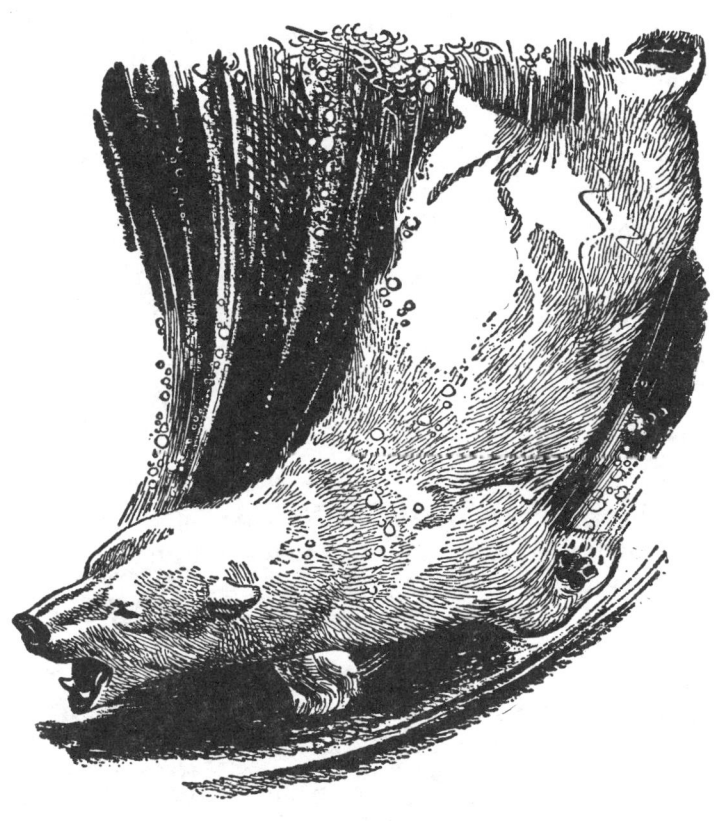

strength with it. Swimming vigorously, Kalak overtook him, although her own breath was nearly gone.
She climbed out of the same lead she had dived

into, and carried the seal up on the ice. Kalak fed heartily, ignoring the little white fox, who patiently waited for her to finish.

Having eaten nothing in days, Kalak slept for only an hour after feasting on the seal's blubber and fat. When she awakened, she strode straight and purposefully across the ice. Now she could finish the task she had set for herself. The Bay of Seals lay in the direction she had taken since leaving the dead whale. Agtuk's village was on the Bay, and hunters from that village had killed her cub. Kalak had not forgotten that, and would not forget. She was going for her revenge.

As they approached the shore, Kalak had a sudden, overpowering desire to eat some grass. She made her way to the shore, followed by the little fox, who patiently sat with his tail curled about his paws as Kalak browsed on withered grass that thrust above the few inches of arctic snow. Kalak raised her head to stare inland, then returned to the ice pack.

A wind rose, blowing hard from the shore out over the pack. The ice buckled and heaved, and long leads opened. Cakes of ice floated about on choppy water, and the heads of seals bobbed among the ice cakes. Even though the sun was not shining, the seals were glad to get out of the water and up on the ice again. They grunted back and forth, napped, and raised their heads every minute or two to look about for danger.

They did not see Kalak. She was again queen of the ice, mistress of her frozen domain, and a hunter whose hunger seemed to know no bounds. She came upon the seals and caught them at the edges of their leads before they were more than aware of her presence.

Kalak feasted, napped, and ate again, but still she was unable to satisfy her enormous hunger. Hunting as she travelled, she continued toward the Bay of Seals. She had no definite time to arrive there because, to her, time meant nothing. Kalak knew only that she much reach the Bay, and after that Agtuk's village.

The little fox waddled contentedly behind her for he too, had grown fat. The fox regarded the plenty which was now his portion as philosophically as he had accepted the lean period when Kalak had been able to catch no seals. He feasted while he could, for before the long night lifted and he was able to make his own living on the arctic shore he was sure to know hunger again.

Kalak came to the Bay of Seals in mid-morning. Now the wind had reversed its direction, and was blasting over the ice toward the shore. It set the pack in motion, ceaselessly opening and closing leads. Ice cakes rammed other ice cakes, and when they could not break or crumble them they heaved themselves on top and rode. The Bay of Seals in winter was even more wild and forlorn than it was in summer.

There were no other polar bears on it; Kalak knew that when she tested the wind. All had left for easier and safer hunting grounds. But, though the Bay of Seals was far from safe, no hunting could be easier at the present. The raging wind kept the ice in motion, and the resulting open water made it simple to get seals.

Kalak caught a seal, ate, and left the rest to the little fox. Then she curled up to sleep, and because the wind still blew from ice to shore, she had no knowledge of the man who saw her and then ran.

Chapter VI

THE DEVIL DRIVER

The devil-driver, Chuesandrin, was in another quandary. He had managed to discover enough charms and portents of one kind or another to convince the villagers that he had had at least as much as Agtuk to do with leading all to the plenty found in the Bay of Seals. Therefore, Chuesandrin's place in the village was again a respected and honored one. He had plenty to eat, and, according to requirements, paid for it by conjuring up or driving away various devils. He had no major worries because, now that his people were safe, even Agtuk tolerated the devil-driver and sometimes half-believed him.

But there were various minor irritations. Hunting was hard work, and hard work was scarcely fitted to the dignity of a devil-driver's position. However, not hunting had definite disadvantages. It was law among the Endorah that any hunter who brought anything down might, if he chose, keep a quarter of it for himself. The remainder was equally divided among the village. Chuesandrin understood the fairness of that arrangement, but he didn't like it.

For, when the hunters chose their portions, invariably they selected the choicest parts for themselves. It had been ten days since Chuesandrin had eaten anything except what somebody else did not want, and such a state of affairs simply could not continue. Chuesandrin liked the tenderest meat and the richest blubber as well as anyone else did.

Now he might have an opportunity to get some. The wife of Toolah, one of the most successful hunters, had come to Chuesandrin with the information that Lueni, one of Toolah's sons, had lost his soul. The boy lay in Toolah's lodge, his head so hot that Toolah's wife was thinking seriously of extinguishing the oil lamp. Lueni was Toolah's favorite son. If Chuesandrin would come see what he could do about the devil that had taken possession of the little boy, Toolah's wife was certain that the devil-driver would not go unrewarded.

After sending her away, Chuesandrin sat for a long while in his own lodge. Devil-drivers came up against many difficult problems, and Chuesandrin had long since learned that his craft was apt to be taken lightly if he reduced his fees to a simple service charge. Therefore he could not simply tell Toolah that he must pay a certain number of oil-filled sealskins and a certain poundage of choice blubber. He had to be more subtle.

Finally Chuesandrin arose, rummaged in his various devil-driving kits, and extracted different kinds of dried herbs which he himself had plucked during the summer. He mixed them carefully, added a little powdered willow root, poured the whole concoction into a stone dish, and filled the dish with seal oil. Chuesandrin stirred with an ivory spoon until the whole mess was evenly dispersed, and poured it into a sealskin.

Carrying the sealskin bag, Chuesandrin crawled out the tunnel that led from his snow house and rose in the arctic gloom. He made his way to the igloo occupied by Toolah and his family, kicked a surly dog out of the way, and knelt to enter Toolah's tunnel. He crawled past the dog harnesses, fishing gear, harpoons, thongs, and other articles which were stored in the tunnel, and arose in Toolah's house.

Lighted and warmed by a fine seal-oil lamp, the house was second in size only to Agtuk's, and as well made. Lueni lay on caribou skins spread across the snow sleeping bench. His eyes were bright and glazed; his face was hot. Toolah came in, and stood anxiously near while Chuesandrin looked about for signs of the devil that had entered Lueni. The devil-driver sighed in relief. There was no rattle in Lueni's chest and his breathing was not labored, therefore his lungs were all right. Obviously the devil had taken possession of his stomach.

"There is a devil in Lueni's stomach," Chuesandrin announced gravely. "He went there to hide, but I can entice him into this sealskin. Then I will take him out and free him on the ice. But I warn you, Toolah, that he may return. It is cold on the ice, but even if this devil freezes so hard that he cannot walk, he can command a polar bear to pick him up and bring him back into the village. If he does, he may hide in Lueni's stomach again unless he is prevented from so doing."

"How may he be prevented?" Toolah asked anxiously.

"I will take one of Lueni's mittens to my lodge.

Thinking that Lueni is there, for I will make a charm
that will cause him to think so, the devil will then enter my lodge. But he cannot for long be deceived. The
devil will stay in my lodge only if he has five skins of
choice seal oil and the best blubber from five of the
fattest seals. Can you furnish that?"

"Yes."

"Carry it to my lodge then, but first give me a mit-
ten and I shall lure the devil out of Lueni."

Chuesandrin knelt, held the sealskin bag to Lueni's
lips, and poured the mixture he had prepared down
the youngster's throat. Lueni squirmed, and muttered
into the sealskin, which Chuesandrin kept firmly over
his mouth. After a few minutes Chuesandrin jerked
the sealskin away and clapped it shut.

"I have the devil!" he chortled. "See! Lueni is cooler
already!"

It was true. Beads of sweat stood on Lueni's fore-
head, but his eyes were no longer glazed. Clutching
the sealskin, Chuesandrin hurried out of the lodge.
He did not know what long-ago devil-driver of the
Endorah had conceived the cure for stomach-ills, but
legend had it that he himself had been sick in the
stomach. Going out from the village, he had watched
various sick animals to see what they ate. Mixing to-

gether all the herbs thus found, he had cured himself and handed the formula for stomach medicine down to his successor. It had been handed on, from devil-driver to devil-driver.

With a bag of seal oil in each hand, Toolah crawled out of the lodge and stood for a moment beside Chuesandrin. He looked respectfully at the devil-driver. Toolah placed his faith in hunting all the time, and if he had to defy devil-drivers in order to get meat for his family then he would do so. But they had their good points.

"Will you take the devil far out on the pack?" Toolah inquired.

"Very far," Chuesandrin assured him. "Have everything I requested ready at my lodge when I return, or else I may not be able to prevent the devil's re-entering Lueni."

"It shall be there."

Chuesandrin started into the arctic gloom. He would now have to walk for some hours, but that was better than poising with a harpoon over a seal's breathing hole for the same length of time. Besides, he liked to walk. As soon as he was out of sight, Chuesandrin looped a thong about his sealskin and slung it carelessly over his shoulder. He grinned. Probably, among the villagers, only he and Agtuk didn't really believe in devils. Appreciating the fact that devil-driving was of genuine value sometimes, Agtuk resented Chuesandrin only when he issued orders that were contrary to the good of all. However, Chuesandrin had finally decided that he had better take care about that. It would not be well to make an enemy of Agtuk.

Three hours after he had left the village, and some miles out on the ice, Chuesandrin stopped. The wind, that had been blowing hard, began to roar. The devil-driver walked a little ways farther, then carelessly threw the sealskin bag down. It was all right to lose a devil on the ice, but he did not necessarily have to face a blizzard in order to do it. Suddenly Chuesandrin stopped in his tracks.

A bare hundred yards away, something moved. Chuesandrin stared. By the stars' dim light he saw a sleeping polar bear. Near-by was a white fox, which stopped feeding to stare at him. The devil-driver slipped silently away and began to run. He ran most of the way to the village, and was panting when he ducked into Agtuk's lodge.

"The devils," he gasped, "are working against us!"

Agtuk said sharply, "You speak to Agtuk now, and not to one of the villagers!"

"True," Chuesandrin grumbled. "And was it not Agtuk who fought with Kalak?"

"Yes." Agtuk's interest quickened.

"She is back," Chuesandrin announced.

"Where?"

"She is back on the Bay," Chuesandrin repeated. "I myself saw her, and I knew her. I cannot forget that you hunters killed her cub, and it is in my mind that she comes to even the score for that killing. I have heard of such things."

"I, too," Agtuk agreed. "The mist bear might attack the village! Send Toolah to me! We must be ready!"

Chuesandrin ran to Toolah's lodge, and crawled in. Toolah glanced at him.

"You will find everything you requested in your lodge," he pointed out.

"Aye, and it is well," Chuesandrin agreed. "I have, however, come to advise you that the devil which was in Lueni has great power. No sooner had I freed him on the ice than he commanded Kalak, the mist bear, to pick him up and bring him back to the village. They are coming now, and though there is no way to prevent the devil from escaping and eating the oil and blubber you furnished, the village can be protected from Kalak."

Toolah sprang up. He paid no more attention to Chuesandrin, but crawled out the tunnel and ran to Agtuk's lodge. Other hunters were summoned, with their dogs and lances.

Wind raged through the village, bearing a few flakes of snow with it. The clouded sky blotted the starlight as Agtuk addressed the assembled hunters.

"Kalak has been sighted on the ice. She may be here any minute. We must either kill her or drive her away; the mist bear cannot be permitted to enter the village. If she comes for the purpose I think, we will not need dogs to seek her out. Take them back to your lodges, and return here."

They waited in the darkness. Snow fell harder. Then the storm abated for a moment and stars shone in the murky sky. The hunters strained forward, gripping their lances. A few dozen feet away, Kalak appeared.

Then, as suddenly as she had come, she was gone.

Chapter VII

DEN IN THE SNOW

As soon as she drew nearer the village, the little white fox became obviously reluctant to follow Kalak any farther. For a way he continued to pad along behind her; Kalak was a good provider and the little fox had no wish to lose a huntress so keen. Then they came very near the village, with its attendant strong smells of men, and dogs, and seal oil, and burning lamps, and refuse, and the fox sat resolutely down. He did not mind facing the ice pack and all its dangers, but it was sheer madness deliberately to enter a village where human beings lived.

Uncaring that her constant shadow had deserted

her, Kalak continued. She smelled Agtuk, Toolah, Nalee, Moostantin, and the others who had taken part in the killing of her cub. The big bear snarled savagely as she strode forward.

She knew that the men awaited her in a body. Without doubt they would be armed. Men were always armed with lances or bows and arrows, or both. Kalak did not hesitate. She, too, was armed with strength and fury. If the men were all assembled in one place, that meant only that she would not have to seek out each individual.

Then, for the first time, she faltered. She stopped, standing perfectly still while driving snow swirled about her and the lashing wind clawed at her white coat. She stood for a few minutes, using her nose to locate exactly every man who faced her.

The snow cleared. Kalak saw the assembled hunters as clearly as they saw her. For a second she faced them, roaring her hate and defiance. Then she whirled and was away, running in the opposite direction as fast as she could go. The opportunity to avenge her cub had presented itself, and strangely, Kalak had not taken it. She had run away.

As soon as she had put a safe distance between the hunters and herself, Kalak stopped again. She stood motionless in the darkness, while wind roared in from the pack and snow pelted her. She swung her head back and forth, testing the wind, while she strove to discover whether or not she was pursued. If so, she would have to run again.

No dog barked. No hunter's scent came to her. Save for the wind's snarl there was no sound. But Kalak jerked her head about.

Twenty feet away, almost invisible in the storm, the little white fox sat with his tail curled about his legs. His was the same friendly manner, the same fawning willingness to do or be anything if Kalak would only let him follow her and live on whatever she did not want of the seals she caught.

Kalak pounced, leaping at the fox so swiftly that her great bulk seemed a cloud of snow blown by the storm. The little fox yelped in amazement and leaped out of the way. Kalak sprang again and again, slapping with her paws, furious in her determination to catch and kill the little creature. She could not, but her intentions were very plain. Crestfallen, filled with sudden fear of this protector he had followed so long, the little fox streaked away into the night. He had understood and forgiven the other time Kalak had tried to catch him, for then she had been hungry. This he could neither understand nor forgive. Kalak was fat and heavy; hunting had been good. And, though the fox knew that he could never be her friend, he had tried in every way he could to be inoffensive. In spite of that he had been ignominiously attacked and cast out. The little fox set off across the ice pack, hoping to find a more reasonable bear to which he might attach himself.

Kalak watched him go, and turned away satisfied. She wanted nothing near her, not even the harmless little fox.

She turned west, loping easily along the shore, with its scant covering of snow, and placing distance between herself and Agtuk's village. She knew the prowess of the Eskimo hunters. Their arrows were swift and their lances sharp. She must put herself beyond the farthest reach of any of the Endorah. Far from seeking them out with the deliberate intention of doing battle, the big ice bear would henceforth be so all-wise and cunning that there would be no possibility of an Eskimo hunter even finding her tracks in the snow.

She travelled steadily for hours, staying on shore because of the many scents that blew in from the ice pack. She did not fear the seals she smelled, but the new mission upon which she had embarked was so delicate and all-important that even the seals might bring harm to her if they knew. Twice, when she scented other bears, she swung much farther inland until their scent was gone. If she had to she would fight, but battle at this time would be only the last desperate resort. She dared take no chances.

Fifty miles from Agtuk's village, the bear finally turned directly inland. The storm gradually subsided. Pale stars flickered above her and lighted the snow-covered way she must travel. Shadowy shapes moved on the snow ahead of her.

Kalak stopped, begrudging the time she needed to do so, but suspicious of these creatures as she had become of everything. They were caribou, a tiny segment of a vast herd that was wintering here, eating lichens. Kalak roared and sprang forward, and the caribou pounded the earth with thudding hooves as they dashed out of her way.

Far from the familiar ice pack, the big bear continued up the shallow gully in which she now found herself. Emerging from it, she met the main herd of caribou, a hundred thousand animals gathered in little bands of from two to fifty and seeming to cover solidly the valley Kalak had chosen. They watched nervously as she passed, and split to give her passageway. The caribou were more curious than alarmed. Polar bears were seldom found so far from the sea lanes, and even more seldom did they hunt caribou. The feeding little bands dropped back and resumed grazing as soon as Kalak passed.

Fretful because she was unable to get away from them, but now pressed for time and lacking a choice, for an hour Kalak made her way through the grazing herd. The little bands became more scattered and fewer in number as she came to the far flank of the herd.

There were wolves here, a horde of big, rapacious killers that were following the caribou. Kalak saw a pack pull down and begin tearing at a bull. Though her hatred for wolves would ordinarily have tempted her to swerve and drive these from their kill, now she went carefully around them.

Far up the valley Kalak found the kind of country she sought. The hills were treeless. The wind that snarled almost constantly about the hills had whisked such snow as had fallen on the heights into the valleys or into sheltered places. The bear approached such a drift, and immediately made ready to retreat if she could but to fight if she must.

The two beasts that faced her in the starlight had

humped their backs and fluffed their fur until they looked much bigger than they were. In the gloom, their bare fangs gleamed startlingly white. They snarled and growled continuously, and made little savage rushes which they always checked when they were less than halfway to Kalak. The pair were barren-ground grizzlies, a mother and her half-grown cub. Having not yet gone into hibernation, they were seeking a suitable den.

Kalak backed away. Unwilling to fight, she was perfectly able to do so if necessary. Probably, if it was a finish fight, she could kill both grizzlies, for she was bigger and stronger. But she had no desire to do battle. She turned and ran, leaving the sheltered drifts to the two grizzlies.

Finally she slowed to a fast walk, a mile-eating pace that took her swiftly into the hills. There was little time left. She must find what she sought very soon, and it must be the right place. At last she reached an area that seemed devoid of all other life. There were no caribou here, no wolves, no musk oxen, not even hares or lemmings.

Kalak climbed another wind-swept hill and travelled around to the drift in its lee. She hesitated for a long while, assuring herself that nothing was near and that nothing had followed. Then she began to burrow into the drift.

She scooped snow until she had penetrated to the grass with which the hill was covered in summer, and then turned around and around until she had trampled a chamber large enough to accommodate her comfortably. She was quiet for a long while, looking through the hole she had made and at the small patch of star-scattered sky she could see beyond it. The wind that screeched around the hill and straight into her burrow carried no scent of anything harmful.

Clouds stole across the sky. The stars were blotted out and soft snow whirled down. Kalak's tension relaxed. The wind was welcome, a friendly thing that whisked more snow around the hill and into the burrow she had scraped. Already the tunnel's mouth was becoming narrow, as more snow piled into it. After an hour the entrance was closed entirely.

Deep under the drift, Kalak lay in a black den of her own making. But it was a cosy den. Bitter cold could find no entrance nor could harsh winds beat in. It was a warm and comfortable place, a fitting nursery for the three tiny cubs which, within four hours after Kalak entered the den, mewled beside her and avidly sought food.

The cubs, two females and one male, were no longer than small rabbits. Their eyes were closed, their ears only pink buds on top of their oddly kitten-like heads. Their feet were curled little stems that seemed far too small for their fat bodies.

Kalak cuddled them softly to her. She nuzzled them and fondled them softly with a paw that was capable of smashing a seal's spine, until the new-born cubs stopped squirming to lie still. Their baby brains were still too young to grasp the significance of their mother's caress, but they could sense her warmth and care. That was enough.

While winter raged outside, and all male polar bears as well as those females without cubs stalked seals on the gloomy ice pack, Kalak lay in the snow den with her cubs. She slept a great deal of the time, but never so soundly that she could not come instantly awake if the wind outside blew a different tone, or one of the cubs whimpered in an abnormal pitch, or if an unusual scent penetrated the den. She had nothing to eat, but now was demonstrated the wisdom of that instinct which had bade her catch and eat as many seals as she could. While crossing from the dead whale to the Bay of Seals, Kalak had eaten three times her normal amount. As a result her body bore an unusually thick coating of fat. She had food in reserve, enough to sustain both herself and the cubs.

And, now that she again had cubs, she again knew fear. Always she had lost her young; never had she reared one to maturity. In the darkness of the winter-locked den, Kalak caressed her three cubs with a deep maternal determination. For them she had fled from the men she hated, had hidden herself away from all other life.

She must not lose them!

Chapter VIII

FIRST LESSONS

In the winter-locked, lightless den, even while she remembered the fate of her other young, Kalak planned ways and means to keep her new-born cubs safe.

Wolves could not harm her but, from this time until they were big enough to defend themselves, the cubs would be at the mercy of a hungry pack or even a hungry wolf. The Eskimo hunters were fierce and relentless; it was not easy for even a mature bear to escape them once they were on the trail. The ice itself was a peril, for one of Kalak's former cubs had been killed by falling ice. Lastly, there was the sputtering launch which travelled faster than the most powerful bear could swim.

In the darkness Kalak stirred fretfully. She needn't fear wolves as long as she stayed near enough the cubs to protect them, but there was always a possibility that one or all of the cubs might stray. If she had to she would fight Eskimos, but they were a terrible enemy whom it was best to avoid. Probably she could protect her cubs from falling ice if she always led them only on paths which seemed safe to her. But she did not know what to do should another launch come; she knew of no defense against such a thing.

She had already decided that she would take her babies far into the pack. Like all polar bears, Kalak was a wanderer. She had ranged fifty or more miles from shore, and knew that good hunting lay in the pack's depths. Moreover, that far out, she had never seen any wolf, Eskimo, or ship. In the far reaches of the pack there was only ice to contend with.

She rose to stretch herself, and the cubs scrambled about her feet as she brushed the den's top with her shaggy back. The top of the den had been snow when Kalak entered, but heat from her own body had melted the snow so that, for a while, water had dripped around her. Then ice had formed on the top and sides, and Kalak and her cubs were locked in an ice-sheath-ed cavern.

The mother bear lay down again, nosing each of the cubs in turn to reassure herself of their presence and safety. She brushed her muzzle across them, lick-ing each cub's back gently.

One of the cubs crawled to her, felt with questing paws, fastened them about Kalak's neck, and bit with baby teeth. Kalak rolled over, careful not to crush the frolicking cub, and grasped it gently with her huge paws. As she played with her cub she grunted ecstat-ically, and the other two cubs joined in. Tiny squeals and excited snarls filled the den.

Kalak got up suddenly, careful to roll the cubs gent-ly from her even as she arose. She thought she had heard something. The den seemed exactly as it had been, but subtle changes were taking place outside and, penetrating beneath the drift where Kalak had denned, had a voice all their own. Kalak stood tensely, her ponderous paws braced. Sensing and reflecting their mother's attitude, the cubs were quiet. Muffled by the intervening snow, the wind's snarling came into the den as a soft and distant hum. The wind was a customary thing, but this time it had a different pitch.

There was no other noise. Kalak lay down again, unworried but restless. She did not drop into one of the prolonged naps which had helped to while away the long hours spent in the den. A great uneasiness possessed her. The den seemed suddenly to have become too small and too warm.

The cubs swarmed over her. Kalak let them play while she listened and waited. All tendency to sleep had departed. She must lie awake because the season was changing, and its sensed change forbade sleeping.

Again Kalak rose to turn restlessly around in the cramped den. She shook herself and, for the first time since she had entered the den, felt hungry. She licked the ice that had formed around the den and ran her long tongue out to lick her chops.

Twenty-four hours later her hunger was a nagging force that would not let her be quiet. Nor could she longer fail to heed the subtle changes outside, the coming of spring. It was time for action.

Kalak rose and strode forward, turning her head aside as she crashed into the wall of the den. A great heap of snow and ice fell about her, but did not close the hole she had smashed. The mother bear stood blinking at the sun, which once more had risen in the sky. She gazed down the hill and across the ragged snow patches at budding grass and shrubs. The wind still blew cold, but spring had definitely come.

Kalak turned to look at the cubs, who crowded past her into the opening she had smashed and looked with awed eyes at the great world that lay beyond them. Their world, as far as they had known it, consisted of a hole under a snow drift. They were afraid of what they saw now, and fearfully slunk back into the den.

Nudging the cubs with her muzzle, pushing them with her paws, she forced them through the door of the den and into the snow outside. The cubs crowded close together for the comfort and feeling of protection they received from each other. Whimpering plaintively, they ran back and sat between their mother's forelegs. Feeling safer there, they pricked up their ears and took a lively interest in a caribou cow that was coming down the opposite hill. The cubs ran delighted tongues out as the cow stopped and bawled. A dozen more caribou followed her down the hill.

Pleading, cajoling, and butting them with her nose when they were very obstinate, Kalak coaxed her cubs farther away from the den. Interest gradually replaced the babies' fear. At first afraid to leave the den, they now followed Kalak, slowly because they were unable all at once to absorb so much that was fascinating. The cubs stopped to investigate dried grass, stones, snow, flowers, patches of dirt, trickles of water, and everything else that lay in their path. They saw no reason to move fast. Their world had been a narrow and restricted den, which was satisfactory enough at the time. But now that fear was gone, and there was so much to see and do, they were in no hurry.

Patiently, and always gently, Kalak led or followed her babies. She never moved more than six feet away and she did not urge them because it was well to ease them gradually into this new realm. To take them bluntly into anything while they were still so small—they were about the size of large cats—might invite danger. The cubs knew nothing about the life they must lead. Until Kalak was able to teach them some arctic lore she must remain doubly cautious.

While the three cubs clustered about an outcropping of rock, and scraped it with their paws, Kalak ate profusely of the dried grass growing on the hillside. The male cub reared with his paws on the rock and bent his tiny head to sniff. He ran his pink tongue out to taste the outcropping, and licked his chops.

Looking around at his mother, the cub came over to taste some grass. He grasped a mouthful, bit it off with baby teeth, chewed slowly, and spat it out. Impatiently asking for more palatable food, he butted his mother's flank.

Kalak obliged, and immediately the other two cubs ran to her. She stretched out in the sun-warmed grass, content but wary. The wind brought her no scent of danger and she could see nothing abnormal, but she dared not relax. She must be ready to repel or evade whatever came.

The mother bear swung her head suddenly, and stood up. Now there was something in the wind, a new scent that had not been there before and more appetizing than dried grass. Eagerly she walked farther down the hill and swung about to await the vanguard of a horde of migrating lemmings.

These small, short-tailed arctic mice were suddenly everywhere. Theirs was a wild and crazy impulse, a mass hysteria that bade them leave the place where they were for another place which they sought only through instinct. Foxes raced at will among them, gulping down as many as they could hold. Owls swooped over the migration, taking what they wished. Wolves, for once finding lazy hunting, moved almost indolently, snapping up the little creatures. Still the mass of lemmings moved on. There was no stopping them and no turning them aside. Those that survived the various meat-eaters who attacked them would continue their migration until they drowned in the polar sea.

Kalak walked to meet them, the cubs following nervously at her heels. This was also something new; until now the living creatures in their world had consisted of their mother, themselves, and the little herd of caribou. The cubs crowded anxiously against their mother's ponderous legs, puzzled by the onslaught of small, living things but not fearing them as long as Kalak stood her ground.

Kalak lowered her head, caught up a lemming, and swallowed it. She ate another, and another, enjoying the first taste of flesh she had had since going into the den. The cub who had taken a mouthful of grass when he saw Kalak doing the same snuffled at a passing lemming, then opened his baby jaws to catch one.

There was an outraged squeal. Bitten on the lip, the cub jerked his head and snapped the lemming away from him. Kalak whirled, roaring and bristling. There was nothing to see except the migrating horde, and nothing to be smelled on the wind. Kalak licked her wounded youngster solicitously and went back to eating lemmings. Her belly filled, she started down the valley. Now the cubs followed her willingly. To them, their mother was all-powerful. They need fear nothing as long as she was with them.

Kalak swung about and headed resolutely for the sea. The lemmings were merely something to stay her appetite until she could reach open water and the seals upon which she was accustomed to feed. Resting when the cubs were no longer able to travel, but pushing them as hard as she could, Kalak came finally to the shore.

High winds and violent storms had already broken the ice at this point. For as far as Kalak could see there was only open water. The big ice bear stopped to ponder. Storms here would also have raged much farther to the west; she was unlikely to find the pack as quickly by travelling west as she was by going east in the direction of Agtuk's village.

However, she was a long way from the village and there was no special risk involved in travelling toward it. Above all, she wished to get her cubs into the safety of the pack. The sooner she was able to do so, the better. Kalak headed east.

Late in the afternoon they reached the ice. Although it was piled high on the shore, there was open water farther out, where the pack ice floated free. Kalak walked out, going around hummocks and ridges which the cubs could not climb over. She came to the lead that separated pack and shore ice.

Kalak dived cleanly, and immediately surfaced to swim beside the ice upon which the cubs remained. Always eager to imitate, the little male belly-splashed into the water, went down, and came sputtering to the surface. He swam in terrified circles, with his paws splashing still more water into his nose. Gradually becoming more at ease in this new element, he settled down to swim gracefully. Delighted grunts burst from him. He circled around and around, demonstrating his prowess for the timid cubs who dared not join him.

The mother bear climbed out on the ice and snuffled at her two babies. Getting behind one of them, she pushed firmly with her muzzle. The cub skidded across the ice, tumbled in, and squalled as the water closed over her head. Kalak pushed the other cub in.

For a few minutes they swam clumsily. Finding their sea legs, they circled more smoothly. Kalak joined them. Side by side, the three cubs swam with her across the open lead.

Nearing the pack ice, Kalak selected a worn place that sloped into the water. Scrambling and raking with their claws, the female cubs scrambled out. The male stared resentfully, then struck out for the ice he had just left. Swimming was a wonderful sport and he wanted more of it.

Stroking easily, Kalak circled around him. She brought up her heavy paw, smack against her disobedient son's fat rear. The cub squalled, described a graceful arc that carried him out of the water and back into it, and squalled a second time. Kalak spanked him again. Obedience was the first law of survival. The cubs must do her bidding and, if they had to learn the hard way that she should be obeyed, then the hard way it would be. The male cub climbed out on the ice and padded meekly along.

From ahead came the rich odor of basking seals.

Now Kalak led the cubs, and when they would have crowded ahead of her she cuffed them back. They followed wonderingly, not able to hide their surprise because a once gentle and indulgent mother had suddenly become so harsh. Never before had she cuffed them. The cubs could not know that, at last, their education was to begin. But they would soon learn.

The scent of seal became stronger, nearer. Kalak

turned as the male cub, who also smelled the enticing scent, tried to rush past. She cuffed him soundly. His more timid sisters stood by and watched. They could and would learn from their brother's punishment. If Kalak did not wish to be passed or crowded, then it was best to respect her wishes.

Kalak read the air currents. There was nothing in them that foretold danger, so she turned and looked at the cubs sternly. Something unheard but not mis-understood passed between them. The cubs remained in a little depression while Kalak went on alone.

She stalked easily, and yet swiftly, for she was com-plete mistress of this kind of hunting. Flat against the ice, motionless when the seal raised its head but slid-ing forward when it napped, Kalak quickly made her kill. She carried the seal back to the cubs, who sniffed interestedly at it and then watched her eat, afterward snuggling against her while she rested on the ice pack.

Kalak led her cubs steadily seaward, but now that she was again on the pack some of her fear and fore-bodings left her. This was ice, and she felt at home on it. Her cubs were safer than they had been on land because only when they could not find caribou did the wolf packs venture into the frozen sea to hunt seals. Nevertheless she could not afford to relax. She

was not yet beyond the limits visited by Eskimo hunters.

The second day out Kalak stopped and swung her
head directly into the wind. She stood a full thirty
seconds, then began to run. When a cub faltered she
nudged it forward with her nose.

Far off she had heard a dog bark, and the wind
brought her the plain scent of the Eskimo hunters who
were with them.

Chapter IX

FLIGHT FROM DANGER

Kalak reared, standing on her hind legs in order to snuffle currents that had been above her when she was on all fours. Very faint and far away, but certainly on the ice pack, the dog barked again. Kalak got the scent of other dogs, and of six men. Among them she identified Agtuk, Toolah, and Nalee. The other three were strangers.

There was another scent, too, that of a mother polar bear with one cub. The pack of dogs broke into full cry. There came the hoarse shout of a man. Kalak dropped back to the ice and looked anxiously at her cubs.

She knew as well as though she were present what was happening across the pack. The men and dogs had struck the fresh trail of the mother bear and her cub. They had followed, and brought their quarry to bay. The mother bear was backed against some hummock or ridge trying desperately to defend her baby while the men closed in with their lances.

Herding the cubs ahead of her, bunting them with her nose whenever they lagged, Kalak started deeper into the pack. She had never met an Eskimo, or even run across a sign of one, more than ten miles from shore. But she was still only halfway to that limit. She should have travelled harder and farther. There would be plenty of time to rest when her cubs were safe in the depths of the pack.

One of the female cubs stopped to lick at the new snow across which they travelled, and Kalak smacked her soundly. The cub skidded sideways into the snow, picked herself up, and ran on. The cubs were fast learning that there would be no arguments with their mother. If they did not do what she wanted done when she wanted it punishment was certain to be swift and severe. In her mind there could be no middle course; the penalty for disobedience might be death.

Across the pack, the cry of howling dogs subsided.

The wind had changed, so that Kalak got neither the scent of the hunters nor that of the dogs. But still she urged them on.

Bigger and stronger than either of his sisters and therefore able to run ahead of them, the male cub had been leading the procession. Suddenly he braced his feet and stopped so suddenly that he almost slid into a cake of ice. In his eagerness to see better, the cub stood up, rearing his small length until he looked like a white teddy bear standing on the ice.

With an immense bound Kalak leaped over her cubs and placed herself in front of them. Her neck was stretched, her head bent. The fur on her back ruffled as she snarled at the intruder who waited calmly beside a hummock.

It was her mate, the big male whom Kalak had last seen in the Bay of Seals. He had been far out on the pack enjoying a lazy and fat winter, but had become tired of isolation and loneliness and set out on another journey. Coolly he stood looking at Kalak and her cubs.

With a gurgling snarl Kalak warned him away. Walking between the cubs and her mate, the female continued toward the farther reaches of the ice pack. After the cubs and mother bear had passed, the mate swung in behind to follow them. He dropped a little farther back when Kalak whirled and snapped at him, but continued to follow. The big male wanted companionship and, even though he was obviously not welcome, he preferred Kalak's company to that of any other bear. He jogged contentedly along, not trying to come any nearer but falling no farther behind. A lonely gull appeared, wheeled over them a few times, and flapped away. Seals slid hastily into the water as they approached.

When Kalak stopped suddenly, the big male halted too. The wind had shifted again, and now was blowing from the shore straight out onto the pack. It carried to Kalak fresh news of the Eskimo hunters and their dogs. She stood a moment more, verifying with her nose the exact location of the hunters. A dog barked. Men yelled.

Kalak swung about to push the cubs forward. The hunters were on her trail and had released their dogs. Kalak had dealt with Eskimo dogs before. She knew their speed, their abilities, and their undeniable courage. She also knew that dogs could run much faster than her small cubs.

She must still try to run away, to find some haven for the cubs before the pack overtook them. There

was nothing else to do. The hunters with their stabbing lances would follow the dogs as closely as possible. If she let herself be overtaken by them, Kalak
knew that she would have little chance. Certainly the
cubs would go down. They were far too young to
defend themselves, and any dog in the onrushing pack
could easily kill all three.

Forced to run too fast and given no rest, the cubs
began to pant. Their pink tongues lolled out as they
gasped for breath. Kalak swung her head to reassure
herself that her mate was keeping his distance, and
butted the cubs harder. No matter what they wished,
they had to run. It would be death to do otherwise.

Ten minutes later the dogs swept upon them.

Led by Natkus, the screaming pack hurtled around
an ice hillock and flung themselves forward. Kalak
herded her cubs toward a spot where she could defend them, while the big male bear was taking the
brunt of the assault. Surrounded by dogs, he swung
his sledge-hammer paws at them.

But the dogs were experienced bear hunters. Those
in front kept well away from the embattled male.
Others dived in from the sides and back. When Kalak's mate whirled to deal with them the dogs that
had been in front attacked.

Kalak waited to see no more. Her mate was momentarily holding the pack. The men were not in sight. She seized the opportunity to drive her cubs farther along in the direction she wished to take them.

They reached an almost level expanse of ice and started across. The wind, swooping across this smooth ice, had whirled the snow from it and made easy going. Hot and resentful, but still running both because they were afraid and because they knew that they would be spanked if they tried to stop, the cubs raced along. Kalak followed, bunting freely with her nose and permitting no lagging.

One of the female cubs was nearly done and could not possibly run much farther. Kalak thrust her nose between her laboring daughter's rear legs and hoisted her skillfully along.

Hope began to struggle with the terror and desperation she felt. Beyond the smooth ice there were more hummocks and ridges, and beyond them she smelled water. She knew that, compared to her, dogs were clumsy swimmers. The hunters could not swim at all. If the lead was big enough she could surely find safety in it.

She heard the pack race out onto the smooth ice and the shrill scream of a stricken dog. Her mate was fighting a running battle and, impeded by the dogs, was falling farther behind. Then Kalak heard the shouts of men. The hunters, coming fast, were almost on the heels of their dogs.

Kalak came to the open lead. Instead of the big water she had hoped to reach, the lead was scarcely fifty yards wide. Merely a rambling pond in the ice pack, it began at a sloping wall of smooth ice, and, a quarter of a mile away, ended at some ragged hummocks. At her feet, a shelf of ice hung a few inches over the water. That was all.

Kalak swung her head to locate the oncoming hunters, and dived cleanly. Unhesitating, the cubs dived with her. They swam side by side, looking to her for guidance, and still did not hesitate when Kalak went under the ice shelf. When she surfaced, only her head broke water but there was room to breathe. Rising beside her, concealed by the ice shelf, the cubs floated quietly.

They heard the scraping of clawed feet on the shelf above them, and saw the big male dive into the lead. Right behind him, the dogs flung themselves into the water and, still yelling, set out after their sighted quarry. Kalak's mate climbed out on the opposite ice pack. Seconds later Natkus and three other dogs had emerged from the lead and were renewing the chase. One by one, as they swam the lead and climbed out, the rest of the pack joined the battle.

Kalak saw her mate scramble to the top of a knoll, and could not miss seeing the red streamlet that flowed down his shoulder. Somewhere on the back trail a dog had leaped in, or a fast-running hunter had come up with the big male and thrust his lance truly. The screaming dogs yelled their fury as they tried to climb up to the top of the knoll.

Then the hunters arrived. The bears heard the soft thudding of their sealskin boots on the ice shelf, and men's voices.

"There's the big one!" cried Toolah. "But what of Kalak, the mist bear, and her three cubs?"

"She has gone on, or again changed herself into mist," another replied. "Come! Let us hurry before more dogs are killed! The big one is a devil in himself!"

The hunters ran around to the near end of the lead and threaded their way among the broken hummocks. Their lances ready, they reappeared on the opposite side of the lead. From the top of his knoll, the male saw them coming and tensed himself. He was a warrior going to his last fight and knew it, but there was no fear within him. A king of the ice, he had run as far as he was going to run.

In an easy little leap, the big bear left the knoll and pounced down among the dogs. Taken by surprise, the pack yelled in fear. A dog flew into the air to fall nearly at the feet of the oncoming hunters. Another skidded out of the pack to lie inert against an ice cake. Yelling hysterically, the rest rallied and flung themselves on both flanks of the enraged male as he charged straight at the hunters.

They thrust home with their lances, but the big bear did not stop. Like a matador measuring a bull for the kill, Agtuk drove his lance deep in the bear's chest. He kept coming, and was almost among the hunters when he finally faltered and sank down on the ice.

Long after the hunters had gone, Kalak led her cubs from beneath the ice shelf. They crossed the lead, climbed out on the ice, and passed the place where their mate and father had died so valiantly. Tarrying only a moment to sniff the bloody ice and snarl savagely, Kalak swung west. She was far out on the ice pack now, and it was unlikely that there would be more hunters, but she must take no chances.

The short spring night had descended when Kalak

finally stopped to catch and eat a seal. She lay on the ice while the cubs snuggled against her and slept. The mother bear dozed only in snatches. Her head was almost constantly up as she searched the wind for danger. The cubs were at the same time her great treasure and her grave responsibility. No matter what happened, they must live.

Chapter X

THE WALRUS HERD

Kalak knew that open water lay south and farther west, that hunters roamed to the southeast, and that the wildest parts of the ice pack stretched as far north as she might walk. She intended to take her cubs deeper into the pack, but wanted to be farther west before starting north. Even though it was unlikely, there was always a possibility of encountering more hunters if she started directly north at this point. So Kalak continued to wander west.

But she was in no hurry. This was a pleasant place in which to linger. A steady northeast wind that never blew strongly still kept the pack from becoming uncomfortably warm. There were plenty of open leads and seals for the taking. Out here, far from shore, the ice was comparatively smooth, with few hummocks or ridges.

There was no lack of food, and the cubs were safe. Because they were, Kalak permitted them more leeway. She never wandered far from her babies and always knew exactly what they were doing and where they were, but there was no longer a need for stern discipline.

Well-fed and healthy, the cubs took advantage of their freedom to indulge in every possible play and antic. Always the little male took the lead; he was the instigator of everything. He remained larger than his sisters, more active, and possessed an insatiable curiosity.

Kalak lay comfortably on a cake of ice and watched her son ramble toward a melted pool that lay among little hillocks. His two sisters, more than ever like animated white teddy bears, followed him, looking back from time to time to assure themselves of their mother's presence.

Kalak raised her head to watch. The male cub was impetuous, prone to rush in first and investigate afterward, and Kalak worried about that tendency in her son because she knew that one day it would lead him into trouble.

However, now he merely walked down to the pool, lapped some water, waded in, and started swimming when he reached a depth too deep for wading. He dived, reappearing ten feet from where he had gone under and looked back at his sisters. They still hesitated, but were unwilling to be left out of the fun. Their brother was having a glorious time, and so far, nothing had appeared to endanger him. The two female cubs rushed to join him.

They swam around and around the pool, diving and rolling, chasing each other and scrambling eagerly with tiny paws and baby jaws as they wrestled. The little male ducked both his sisters, then was set upon by both, and struck out for the edge of the pool.

The male cub scrambled out of the water, ascended a sloping ridge, and stood looking down at his sisters. Letting himself go, he rolled his butter-fat body down the slope and splashed into the pool. Immediately he swam back and climbed the same slope. Again he slid into the pool. After watching him a moment, and learning the technique of ice sliding, his sisters joined in. Sometimes singly, and sometimes tumbling together, the three rolled and splashed into the pool.

Finally, tired and hungry, they climbed out and pounced upon Kalak. She rolled over to let them feed, and tumbled the little male gently between her paws. He seldom remained tired for long, and was usually in a mood for more play. Presently he, too, sighed, yawned, and lay down to sleep with his sisters.

After a while Kalak got up and went forth to hunt. She had taught the cubs to stay where she left them while she stalked seals, and no longer had to worry about them. She still did not like to get too far away, and as a consequence she had to choose her seals with care.

Presently she located a seal lying beside an open lead just beyond the pressure ridge that concealed the cubs. Carefully, not showing herself and making absolutely no noise, she slunk across the ice. Kalak had done this so many times that it was routine, and experience had given her a hunter's knowledge of what to expect.

She knew that she would catch this seal. It was five feet from the edge of the ice, and not over-cautious. Raising its head every minute or two, it would look lackadaisically about and then go back to sleep. Kalak advanced swiftly to an easy kill.

Then, almost as she was ready to strike, the male

cub scooted past her, straight at the seal. Wriggling as easily as though it were sliding on oil, the seal slipped into the water and dived. The male cub stood open-mouthed, staring in perplexity at the spreading ripples that rolled across the surface of the water.

The next second he tried frantically to run, but was too late. Roaring her anger, scolding her son in every way she knew, Kalak was upon him. She raised a huge forepaw and spanked him smartly. Again and again she struck, bringing the flat of her paw across her son's fat rear. Bawling, he raced back to his sisters. Kalak raised her paw to strike again, thought better of it, grunted sourly, and moved off to find another seal.

She made a kill, ate, and watched the scavenging gulls swoop to what was left when she lay down to sleep. Her chastised cub crawled humbly up to her and snuggled down with his two sisters.

Always Kalak worked westward. As soon as she had gone far enough she would swing north. There was an area there, fifty miles wide by a hundred miles long, where the pack ice moved just enough to keep leads open all winter. Seals were abundant, because the water beneath the ice was choked with shrimp and fish. No human hunter had ever gone there.

Kalak had that place in mind as an adequate school for her cubs. They would have space in which to gratify the polar bear's natural tendency to wander. There would be plenty of food, and no enemies. Day by day Kalak travelled toward that haven.

Finally they came to the edge of the ice and the beginning of open sea. Wave-topped water rolled ahead, and lapped the irregular line of ice. Ice cakes of varying sizes tossed about in the sea.

Kalak swung northwest, following the sea line but keeping back from the water. Eventually, she neither knew nor particularly cared when, she would reach unbroken ice where nothing except seals and polar bears could venture.

Seals were plentiful here and Kalak went out to hunt one. As soon as she departed, the male cub left his timid sisters and started in a direction opposite to that taken by Kalak. He had smarted too much and too long to again risk spoiling one of Kalak's hunts, but he could go hunting by himself.

On the edge of the ice, very near the sea, the cub stopped to look. Lying on the ice and playing in the water just ahead of him was a herd of walrus. The cub looked hesitantly at the huge bull and the great cows, and stared back toward his sisters. Then he caught sight of several calves among the walrus herd and his confidence returned. He might not be able to catch a big one, but surely he could bring down one of the smaller ones. Cocksure, secure in his own opinion of himself, the cub stalked a walrus calf.

He pounced upon it and sank his claws into its hide while he tried to bite with baby teeth. The startled calf, dragging the cub with it, struggled toward its angered mother. Lumbering over the ice, she struck out with one of her great flippers. The cub's breath was forced from him in one great gasp and he was knocked into the sea. One by one, splashing prodigiously, the rest of the walrus herd slid into the water.

Thoroughly aroused, knowing that one of the calves had been in danger, the old bull charged toward the cub.

Kalak stalked and killed her seal, and carried it back to the place where she had left her cubs. Instant panic seized her. All three cubs had been here when she left, but now the male was gone. Kalak dropped the seal and, with her nose to the ice, loped swiftly along on her youngster's trail.

She raised her head to see the walrus herd, and her cub within half a yard of one of the calves. He pounced upon it, clinging with baby claws and teeth as the little walrus instinctively struggled toward its mother. Kalak saw the mother come to the rescue, and she watched the cub hurtle into the sea.

Before the cub struck the water, Kalak was running. Her reflexes and reactions were so swift that she needed only a split second's pause on the edge of the ice to grasp the situation.

Kalak sprang from the ice, and landed exactly in the short and rapidly closing space between her cub and the charging bull. Even as she struck the water, she turned to fling out her claws and fight.

They came together, the enraged bull who was fighting for his herd and the mother bear who would battle to the death for her baby. Kalak sank her claws deep into the bull's wrinkled skin, and sought for a hold with her jaws. She found one in the short, fat neck, and felt her fangs sink deep into leathery skin and flesh. The bull turned to wriggle away.

As soon as he did, Kalak relaxed her hold and let him go. Pivoting in the water, she swam back to her cub. Still half senseless, gasping for breath, he paddled weakly on the surface and strove toward the ice. Kalak pushed him with her nose, then turned back to face the enraged herd.

She could see walrus all about. Monstrous things, some of which outweighed her by half a ton, they made a half circle in the water and slowly closed in. The big bull's flabby lips quivered. He raised out of the water, his tusks gleaming in the sun, and bellowed his challenge.

Kalak glanced briefly about, and saw the cub still making his painful way toward the ice. He had almost reached it, but before he did she would have to withstand the charge of the walrus herd.

The big bull dribbled water-thinned blood from the scratches and bites Kalak had inflicted, while his rage mounted. He had not wanted this fight, but now that he was committed to it he would see it through. The bull lunged forward.

Slipping to one side, Kalak fastened her claws in his neck and rode with him. The rest of the herd closed in. Kalak felt a great blow on her ribs, and an agonizing pain in her chest. She relinquished her hold on the bull to float breathlessly, then had to dodge as another walrus charged her. She looked about and saw the cub climbing up on the ice.

Treading water warily, facing the herd, Kalak backed toward the ice shelf. She reached it, and turned around to draw herself up. As she did so the bull

smashed at her again. One of his tusks left a gaping wound in her left rear leg.

Safe on the ice, Kalak whirled to snarl at her tormentors. Out in the sea, the walrus herd rode in the water and stared at her with lusterless eyes. Kalak waited a moment more; perhaps they would try to come up on the ice and renew the battle.

They did not come and Kalak turned away to inspect her cub. Bruised and breathless, badly scared, he shivered on the ice, staring wide-eyed at the walrus herd. The cub sidled up to Kalak, and whimpered. Kalak licked his fur, comforting him with her tongue and making no attempt to punish him. Obviously the cub had already been punished enough.

Kalak glanced again at the walrus herd. Ugly, ungainly beasts, they waited just off the ice and bobbed up and down in the little swell that rolled in. They had not sought trouble, and would fight only when it was forced upon them. Now they waited to see if Kalak would renew her attack.

She did not. Hers had been a rescue mission only and, now that she had accomplished it, she was satisfied. Kalak bent her big head around to her own side, and winced. There was a stabbing pain in her right chest, and a harsh grating of broken bones. Her rear leg bled profusely, spilling a red trail on the ice, but already the cold was beginning to stop the bleeding.

With the one cub walking meekly beside her, Kalak limped back to the other two. She could not know that four of her right ribs were broken, or that the charging walrus' stabbing tusk had barely missed a lung. She only knew that she and the cub were both alive, and her family together again.

Kalak lay down on her left side and the cubs crowded close to her. The two females, who seemed to sense that near-tragedy had occurred, whimpered softly. Kalak comforted them with her tongue, and bore her pain stoically.

The wind moaned over the ice pack. The sky clouded and a soft snow fell. The two female cubs stopped whimpering and slept. Their brother lay beside them, wide-eyed and awed at what had happened. He had learned. The world was an exciting and wonderful place, but there were some things in it better left alone. Never again would he stalk or even go near a walrus of any description. Hereafter, until he was sufficiently old and wise to look after himself, he would look to his mother for everything he needed.

Kalak finally rose stiffly and, limping, led her cubs northward along the arctic sea. Had she been alone she might have rested until she was strong and well, and until her smashed ribs knitted. But she was not alone, and the cubs had to eat. They could not do so unless she did.

Kalak left the cubs in hiding and stalked a seal, but she was no longer the perfect huntress she had been. She could not lie flat on the ice and hitch herself along; the broken ribs on her right side forbade that. Kalak was still yards from the seal when it saw her and glided into the water.

Again and a third time, she tried and failed to catch a seal. Hunger gnawed at her. She returned and fed the cubs, then rose to stalk again.

It was no use. She could not crawl stealthily enough, or hide herself well enough, to get near the alert seals. There was no other food; only seals, polar bears, and an occasional herd of walrus ventured into this lonely, ice-locked world. There was not even grass which she might eat. At the next feeding the cubs found little food, and began to whimper. They tried to feed again, but there was nothing for them. The surly little male, who had been the cause of it all, laid his ears back and spat like a kitten at his sisters. The two females crouched close to Kalak's side, and looked at their brother with puzzled eyes. They had learned much in their short lives, but this was the first time they had been hungry.

Kalak tried for still another seal. Crawling along, inching herself slowly across the ice, she stalked as carefully and as well as she knew how. Never once did she avert her eyes from the seal she was after. When her quarry raised its head, she stopped. While the seal napped, Kalak advanced. She came within pouncing distance and sprang.

Kalak brought her paw down on the seal, and searing pain wracked her whole body. Unable to strike hard enough, she did not kill her quarry and the seal squirmed from under her pinioning paw.

The mother bear returned to her babies. The cubs crowded over her, looking for the milk they had always found but which, strangely, was not present now. Kalak raised her head to test the wind, and struggled to her feet.

She left the open sea to start back east, toward the center of the pack. Puzzled, the cubs crowded her heels. Disregarding the pain each step caused her, Kalak walked faster.

There was no food that she was able to catch in this land of ice, but there were other polar bears. Kalak had smelled one, and was going in search of it.

After a few miles, the male cub stopped suddenly, nose twitching. He had scented what Kalak had known she would find, a half-eaten seal. Wandering over the ice with no special destination in mind, the other polar bear was finding good hunting. He feasted on whatever he wanted of the blubber and fat and left the remainder on the ice. Kalak came to such a kill, and growled at the flapping gulls that had settled around it.

The seal was frozen, and consisted only of what the male bear had not wanted, but it was food. Kalak crushed the frozen bones with her jaws and ate them, too. Presently, when she had finished eating and lay down, there was again milk for the cubs.

For more than a week she followed the other bear, eating his discarded kills while her hurt body mended. Then, after a while, Kalak found she could hunt again. She stalked a seal from the water, and killed it in its basking place on the ice. Kalak feasted, then led her cubs back to the west. She did not fear now; she could again provide for her family.

Chapter XI

AGTUK THE HUNTER

Agtuk, Chief of the Endorah, was very dissatisfied. Supposedly he was the best hunter of his tribe and one who knew more arctic lore than any other. In truth, there were no others who could match his prowess; Agtuk accepted that with the modesty which befitted a chief. But none knew better than he that his strength and skill did not always prevail.

Twice had he met Kalak, the mist bear, face to face, and once he had even wounded her. He did not blame himself for failing to kill her the first time, for certainly it was not his fault because the ice had broken away and carried Kalak into the sea. But the next time Kalak had walked right into the village and Agtuk hadn't even flicked his lance at her. Now, he felt, she had eluded him a third time. He should have been able to corner her and her three cubs, or run her down with the dogs. But she had simply disappeared.

As he helped skin one of the seven bears the hunting party had brought down, Agtuk meditated on these failures. Kalak was not an ordinary bear, and no ordinary hunter need feel shame when she escaped him. But he, Agtuk, was not an ordinary hunter, either. As he worked, Agtuk communicated his thoughts to Toolah.

"I have been thinking much of Kalak," he admitted. "I blame myself for not getting her while she was within reach."

Toolah shrugged. "Kalak is a mist bear," he said simply. "Nobody may be blamed for not killing a bear which can at will change herself into mist and float away."

Agtuk said grimly, "And neither can a hunter be blamed for doubting some of Chuesandrin's fancies. There is no such thing as a mist bear."

"Then what is she?"

"A great and wise ice bear," Agtuk said positively. "When we came up with her the first time, she might have escaped had she not wished to defend her young. When she came to the village in the dead of winter, the second time, she was bent upon revenge. I do not know how she recovered from the wound I gave her, but she did. I think she ran away the second time because the birth of her present cubs was near. Yesterday, when we chased her across the ice, she was cunning enough to keep her young safe once more. I wish now that I had looked under the shelf of ice that overhung the lead where the big bear was killed. At the time I never thought of it."

"Do you think she was under there?" Toolah asked in surprise.

"I am sure only that she was somewhere near-by," Agtuk admitted. "I wish I had been able to catch her. Everything would have been better."

"Why?" Toolah asked. "We have seven bears now."

"Because of Chuesandrin. Our devil-driver does much good because he knows many secret potions to make a sick person well. But he wishes to have complete control of the village and to make even Agtuk answer to him. At present he cannot do it because our people have plenty and they are not hungry. What of the next time food is scarce?"

"I do not understand," Toolah said.

"Chuesandrin is very clever," said Agtuk. "He uses his charms as a hunter uses lances and harpoons, only he works upon thoughts rather than the body. When people are in want, and desperate, their minds are easy targets for Chuesandrin's weapons. The next time we find poor hunting, Chuesandrin will remind the village that I met Kalak twice and was hot upon her trail a third time. That time she had three small cubs. Chuesandrin will tell hungry people that Agtuk, who professes to lead them, cannot even catch a polar bear cub. With hunger gnawing at their bellies, the villagers may turn to him, for they will know that he speaks the truth."

"Is that all that troubles you?" Toolah asked shrewdly.

"No," Agtuk confessed. "I have another reason for wishing I had again met Kalak. She killed one of our hunters. I lead the village, Toolah, and I am glad to do so. But a chief should be able to overcome a polar bear, however cunning. For my own peace of mind I wish to find Kalak."

"When are you leaving?" Toolah asked quietly.

"At once."

"It will be a difficult hunt," Toolah pointed out. "All polar bears are far-wanderers. To find one on the ice pack, especially at this time of year, will not be an easy matter."

"Kalak has cubs," Agtuk said. "I think she intends to lead them to some place where they will never meet hunters. Therefore she will certainly take them to the northwest, and I will find them out on the ice. Once she leads her cubs to what she considers a safe place, Kalak will stay there."

"Spring travel is not good," Toolah objected.

"It is not the best," Agtuk conceded, "but I have travelled on spring ice before."

"How far out do you expect to find her?"

"I do not know."

Toolah hesitated. When he finally spoke, his voice was low.

"I do not like to speak of this," he muttered. "You are our Chief, and it is not for me to speak. But Chuesandrin says that there are many devils far out on the ice."

Agtuk laughed. "Chuesandrin's devils are everywhere. But I have seen none of them when he was not also there. Do not fear for me, Toolah."

He sheathed his knife, looked down at the limp skin of the polar bear, and kicked thoughtfully at a piece of ice with the toe of his sealskin boot. Natkus sidled up to him, and Agtuk reached down to scratch the big dog's ears. He looked toward the west, and said slowly,

"When you get back to the village, Toolah, make certain that Larensa gets her share of these polar bear skins and such meat as she wishes. Tell her that I have started on the trail of the mist bear, but that I will return in time for the caribou hunts."

"Good hunting," Toolah said gravely.

"And good hunting to you," Agtuk replied.

With Natkus padding beside him, he started toward the skin tent that the hunters had erected on the ice. Agtuk caught up his bow and arrows, tested his lances, and fastened the best one to the pack that he rolled in a caribou skin. Properly, he should travel either in a kayak or with a dog sledge. But this was spring. The water would not be sufficiently open to permit kayak travel, and there would be enough water on top of the ice so that travelling with a team and a sledge might be awkward. He would go lightly burdened.

With no backward look at the camp he set off across the ice. When he came to the place where they had cornered and killed Kalak's mate, he looked understandingly at the shelf of ice beside the open lead. Kalak was indeed all-wise and all-cunning. Instead of swimming the lead, in full view of the dogs, she had probably lingered under the ice when they came up. Agtuk grinned faintly. This was the sort of strategy he could appreciate and understand. He matched himself against a truly great foe.

Agtuk squatted on the ice, and looked westward. When he was a squalling baby in his fur cradle, a polar bear had snuffled up to the snow house in which he had been born. It had tried to break in, and Agtuk's father had killed it with a lance.

His knowledge of polar bears had begun there, and increased ever since. He knew their mannerisms and their habits—almost the intricate processes of their minds. Also, he understood the difference in bears. No two thought or acted alike any more than Agtuk and Toolah, or Chuesandrin and Nalee, thought and acted in the same way. A primitive being himself, Agtuk understood the workings of other primitive minds. He stopped to consider.

When the Endorah Eskimo brought in a whale, he was always careful to pour fresh water over its head in order that other whales might not take offense and remain forever out of harpoon range. Agtuk knew the true significance of that ceremony. The Endorah had to live on the creatures about them, and they could appreciate those creatures. They were living, breathing things which differed from the Eskimos only in degree and shape. They must be treated with respect.

Larensa loved her son, so it must follow that Kalak loved her cubs. Perhaps she did not love or think of them in the same fashion, but she would try to keep them from harm.

With the point of his knife Agtuk traced a little design on the ice. Then he rose to go on.

Somewhere in the depths of the pack he would again find Kalak. She would try to hide her young, and Agtuk would do his best to ferret out that hiding place. If Kalak was the mightiest bear, he was the mightiest hunter. The issue between them must be settled.

Natkus found a seal's breathing hole. With his short lance in his hand, Agtuk squatted patiently over the hole until the rising seal pushed up his ivory bobber. Agtuk thrust, felt his lance strike home, and held on with both hands. When the seal had ceased struggling he chipped ice until the hole was big enough to draw his dinner out of its aquatic lair. Agtuk and Natkus feasted, then slept.

They went steadily on, Agtuk aware but heedless of the fact that they were farther out on the ice than any man and dog of the Endorah had ever before ventured. When they were tired they slept, and when they were hungry, Natkus smelled out another seal and Agtuk caught it. He made no deliberate effort to follow exactly in Kalak's path, but he knew he was right. Twice during the long trek he found the unmistakable tracks of a polar bear and three cubs. He had guessed correctly, and his own innate knowledge of polar bears and their habits was standing him in good stead. Kalak was taking her cubs exactly where he had thought she would take them.

Agtuk travelled fast, and on the sixth day after leaving the camp where he and his comrades had hunted, he came to open sea. The Eskimo stared wonderingly across it. This was unfamiliar water, a part of the ocean he had never before visited. Neither, he felt with a little touch of pride, had any other man of the Endorah. Agtuk had travelled farther than any man of his tribe.

And somewhere he knew that Kalak awaited him. That had to be, for the meeting was fated. But where was she?

He pondered only a moment. Kalak would not have

swung south, for that way lay danger to her cubs. Throughout his life Agtuk had heard rumors of other hunters who lived along this coast. Certainly Kalak would not risk meeting them. To the east were the hunters of the Endorah, and to the west was water far too large for even a bear of Kalak's skill and daring. Surely she would not venture into it with three cubs at her heels. She had to travel north.

Agtuk followed the sea lane north. Now, when he stopped to eat or sleep, he always looked to the hunting heads on his arrows and lance. He was on the right trail. The decision between himself and Kalak could not be too long delayed. Soon the whole north would know which was the mightiest and most courageous hunter. It had to be Kalak or Agtuk. It could not be both.

Trotting a little way ahead, Natkus stopped and bristled. Agtuk halted, shading his eyes with his hand as he inspected the little herd of walrus on the ice a-head. Slowly he walked on, as the cumbersome beasts slid into the water. They surfaced a little way out, swimming about and grunting angrily at him.'Agtuk ignored them; walrus would attack people only when they themselves were attacked. He stopped where the herd had been basking, and looked about.

As the season advanced, the sun came up earlier and stayed later. The rising sun melted the ice, so that there were little pools and lakes on top of the pack. Many times had Agtuk and Natkus been forced to go through or around them.

At this point, the basking place of the walrus herd, the sun had melted the ice without eliminating the tracks of a big polar bear and those of a small cub. Agtuk guessed what had happened. Somehow, one of Kalak's cubs had fallen in with the walrus herd. Going to rescue it, Kalak herself had been injured. The blood trail she left was still plain on the ice. Agtuk followed it for a way, and found where Kalak had lain down with her cubs. There was little blood there, and no sign of a struggle.

Agtuk nocked an arrow, let it fly at a wheeling gull, and watched the transfixed bird come fluttering down. The Eskimo fired his seal-oil lamp, and cooked the gull. He ate, and fed Natkus the remains.

Patience was a hunter's virtue; nobody understood its value as well as a hunter did. And Agtuk would need patience now. Obviously Kalak was too badly hurt to hunt for herself, and she had three cubs to feed. She must have food, and could get what she needed only by finding another bear and taking what remained of his kills. One of two things had to happen; either Kalak would be unable to find another bear and get food, or she would find one.

If the first, then she would die on the ice and her cubs would starve. If the second, she would swing back to the line of march she had been following. It was as well to await her right here. Even if he wished to do so, Agtuk knew that he could not unravel all the wanderings Kalak might pursue when sick and wounded. Besides, it ill-behooved a hunter to pit himself against a sick bear. When the fight came about, it must be fair. Agtuk would not go back to the village and say that he had overcome a wounded bear.

Much of the snow had melted, but in the sheltered lee of an ice hummock Agtuk found a drift. With his long knife he hacked blocks out of it, laid them in a circle on a firm area of ice, and piled more blocks on top. He closed the top, fashioned a tunnel, and had a windproof snow house. Agtuk next made a snow sleeping bench, and laid his caribou skins on it. He arranged his oil lamp so that he could both cook upon it and heat his house.

He was in no hurry and could afford to wait. By this time the entire village knew that Agtuk had gone to seek the mist bear. When and if he returned to the village, it must be with definite knowledge about the fate of Kalak. If she had died on the ice, Agtuk had to know. If he was able to overtake and fight her, then he must return with some token that he had battled the mist bear. Whatever Agtuk reported, he would be believed because he was a hunter and a chief. None would doubt him.

For two more days Agtuk wandered north. As he travelled, the sea lane he followed grew progressively narrower. Though he could not see the ice on the other side, sometimes, when the sun was at its height, he could see it reflecting from that ice. Somewhere up ahead the lead would become narrower still, and then there would be only ice.

Finally, near the shore he again found the tracks of Kalak and her three cubs. The bear had killed a seal very recently, Agtuk discovered, and had eaten a portion of it. The Eskimo tested his bow string to be certain that that was in proper working order, and looked to his lancehead. Then he began to search through the ice hummocks among which he found himself. It was not an ideal place in which to meet Kalak, but if he must meet her here he would be ready.

Natkus ran to the edge of the ice and snarled. Agtuk whirled, and gasped in astonishment.

Instead of the bear he had expected to see emerging from the ocean, Agtuk saw a ship. Her masts were bare and the sails furled. Black coal smoke poured from her stacks. If Agtuk had not been too awe-stricken, he would have run. As it was, he could only stare.

At one time or another he had heard of these oomiaks larger than the largest whale, but until now he had always considered them the product of someone's imagination. Now he saw for himself that they were not. They were real, and Agtuk shook an astonished head. Then he nocked an arrow, leaned his lance against a convenient hummock, and prepared to defend himself. He was still a hunter, and a chief.

A smaller oomiak with men in it had detached itself from the back of the great one. Sputtering noisily, leaving a curling wake behind it, it snorted toward him. Agtuk drew the arrow to its feather, then lowered his bow and waited. He would fight as hard as he could if he must, and if he fell he would fall fighting. But he had no quarrel with the men who came in this strange craft. If they were enemies, then let them prove it. They could strike the first blow.

The launch hove to and an Eskimo in the bow called out in a dialect which Agtuk understood,

"What do you do here?"

"I hunt," Agtuk answered. "I seek Kalak, the mist bear."

The Eskimo spoke some strange gibberish to the three other men in the boat. Agtuk looked wonderingly at them. They were heavily bearded men who wore garments strange to his land, garments Agtuk thought very clumsy. The Eskimo called back,

"What is the mist bear?"

Agtuk asked contemptuously, "And where do you come from, that you do not know?"

"We are strangers who have sailed many days to get here. We do not know of this mist bear."

Agtuk thawed; strangers could not be expected to know important things and he must be courteous.

"She is the greatest of all bears," he said. "Three times has she escaped me, she and her cubs."

"You say she has cubs?"

"Three of them."

"Do you know whither she goes?"

Agtuk waved an arm northward. "She follows the ice to the north, where she hopes to escape in the pack. I follow her, for I must battle the mist bear again, to prove that I am a worthy chief of the Endorah."

"We seek cubs," the Eskimo declared. "Will you ride with us, and show us where this mist bear goes?"

Agtuk hesitated. Since coming to this great water he had longed for a kayak. Now, even though he was a little afraid of it, here was an opportunity to ride in the biggest craft he had ever seen. Agtuk again looked to his weapons. He was chief of the Endorah, and as chief he feared nothing.

"Yes," he called. "Natkus and I will ride with you."

Chapter XII

THE LAST MEETING

For the first time in many days, Kalak felt easy and relaxed. The three cubs, growing almost noticeably larger and stronger as each day passed, walked beside or behind her as she travelled, or frisked off on small expeditions of their own. Kalak let them go.

Anything but expert hunters, not yet nearly large enough or experienced enough to take care of themselves, the cubs were by no means the tiny things which she had led out onto the ice. And, as they travelled, they had discovered some of the facts of their arctic life. Even the seals might be dangerous.

The male cub had learned that very forcibly only

three days ago. Coming by accident between a seal and the nearest water into which it could slide, he had galloped happily in for the kill. However, hunting seals was not as simple as it always appeared to be when his mother hunted.

Confronted by a bear cub less than half its own size and weight, the seal had shown fight. Rising on its flippers, it had bitten viciously at the cub. Almost turning a somersault in his efforts to get out of the way, the astonished little bear had skidded out of danger just in time. From a safe distance he had watched Kalak come up out of the water, kill the seal with one blow of her paw, and had then helped eat it.

Through such experiences, the cubs were learning, little by little, the things they must know to survive. Kalak was feeling more and more relaxed partly because her most troublesome cub seemed at last to be substituting common sense for enthusiasm, and partly because the greatest dangers she knew were rapidly being left far behind.

She herself had met and almost exterminated the preying wolf pack; there were none out here at all. She had met and eluded the Eskimo hunters, and had proven to herself that she knew how to lead her three cubs among safe ice-ways. Soon they would be deep in the pack. Every day saw them nearing the region where Kalak had wished to enter.

Stretching hundreds of miles to the south and west where she had first come upon it, the sea lane she followed was fast becoming so narrow that she was almost able to see the ice on the other side. Had she possessed the vision of a human being, rather than the weak eyes of a bear, she could have seen it. Less than three miles of water lapped between the ice lanes. And only a few miles north, open water ended at a perpetually frozen sea.

With the cubs curled against her, Kalak lay down to sleep. Almost within the haven she wanted to reach, she dozed peacefully. She stirred when the male cub finally got up and went forth to snuffle at something that had interested him, but it was not that which had awakened her. The cub was safe in this place. It was something else.

Deep within the ice-locked area where she cuddled her babies, some master tuning-fork had struck a note. It throbbed across the ice, humming from ridge to hummock and across crevices. It rolled along smooth ice, flowed over open leads, and vibrated through the broken ice fields. Because Kalak was a wild creature, always in perfect harmony with whatever happened in her world of ice, she felt it too. A storm was coming.

She rose, and glanced about uneasily. The various ice formations hadn't changed; the sky remained as it had been, the soft wind retained a constant note. To all outward appearances, everything was as it had been.

Still the note had come, the thrill had been felt, and because of that Kalak was restless.

Roused from deep slumber, the female cubs wriggled protestingly. They got up, stretched, and showed their pink tongues as they yawned. They sensed nothing unusual. Neither did the male cub, who wandered back padding confidently across the ice, black eyes gleaming as he brushed the ice with his nose in an effort to discover something else that might be interesting.

Kalak remained alert, looking about as though for a visible enemy which might appear at any moment. Suddenly she started across the ice.

The cubs followed, trailing at her heels and looking about as though now they, too, had an inkling of something impending. They were only sensing and reflecting their mother's attitude, but that was enough; the cubs were learning the hair-trigger reactions of wild things. Even the male made no move to stray.

Kalak led her cubs down to the sea. There she raised her head, snuffling the wind and looking all around. There was nothing to be smelled and nothing unusual to be seen.

Just ahead, the ice-invading sea arm she had been following bent its elbow in a westerly direction.

A covey of frightened clouds scudded across the sky. Again the tremor came, not audible and not felt, but surely sensed. Kalak led her cubs at a fast lope up comparatively level ice on the edge of the sea.

Around the elbow, the water narrowed abruptly. Kalak looked across at the low ice hills on the other side. She plunged into the water, made certain that her cubs were beside her, and started to swim.

To Agtuk the ship *Narwhal* was a world so new and amazing that it might have been conceived in one of Chuesandrin's wildest dreams. Indeed, so bizarre were some of the things about him, that not even Chuesandrin could have dreamed them up.

There were no oars or paddles, but the *Narwhal* still moved. Though he had never before believed in devils, Agtuk was tempted to do so now. Somehow the men on this great oomiak must have harnessed a devil to push their boat so fast and so efficiently.

Agtuk asked no questions because he knew that to do so would only betray his own ignorance. However, he could look. He walked to the stern of the ship and peered over at the churning wake left by the propeller. Agtuk revised some of his opinions. Obviously the whirling blades kept the ship moving. In turn, the propeller must be moved by some device deep in the bowels of the ship.

The Eskimo who had questioned Agtuk came to stand beside him.

"Is it not strange?" he asked.

"It is strange to me," Agtuk admitted honestly. "What makes it go?"

"I do not know myself," the Eskimo confessed, "except that there is a metal monster inside which eats coal, and gets very hot."

"Why do these men bring their oomiak here?" Agtuk inquired.

"Every year some of them come to my village. They catch whales, they kill seals, they hunt walrus. It is the purpose of this one to take live cubs of the polar bear."

Agtuk knitted a puzzled brow. "They must come from a very poor land," he observed. "Even though they know how to build a thing like this. And so large an oomiak for the purpose of catching bear cubs is surely a waste of time. Polar bear is not the best of eating, and there would not be enough meat on even a great many cubs to feed these men for very long. I do not understand it."

A herd of seals appeared on the ice. As the *Narwhal* curved in toward them, men appeared on the deck, and Agtuk watched them curiously. Apparently they wished to take seals, but had nothing with them except some odd-shaped sticks. Agtuk smiled. The bearded men on the ship surely knew how to handle her, but just as surely they knew little about arctic lore. That they should hope to kill seals by pointing sticks at them—

The rifles roared and, while Natkus cringed at his side, Agtuk covered his ears to muffle the great noise. He looked wonderingly at the seal herd. Most were sliding across the ice and diving into the water, but some remained where they were. Astonished, Agtuk looked at the blood-stained ice upon which they lay. He could not conceal his bewilderment. But he said nothing. A chief of the Endorah was not a child, to ask questions about things he did not understand.

"The weapons are called rifles," the Eskimo who had come with the ship announced. "They throw little pieces of metal great distances, and very hard." He added casually, "When this voyage is over I am to have one. Thus do the white men give gifts to my tribe."

Agtuk made no comment. Obviously the white men who owned the ship had some wonderful things, but could a man call himself a hunter if he was unable to get his own game with a knife, lance, or a bow and arrows? Agtuk wondered. The men of the Endorah were lazy enough as it was when game was plentiful and easy to get. If they had only to point one of these things . . . Agtuk shook his head. If the Endorah ever got such weapons, they would hunt only a little of the time and then sit in their igloos. They would no longer be a tribe of hunters; the women might just as well take over.

"Perhaps," the Eskimo suggested, "you may have such a weapon yourself if you lead us to polar bear cubs."

"I already have fine weapons," Agtuk murmured. "Here are a lance, a knife, and a bow and arrow. I know what is in them, and what they will do, because I made them with my own hands from materials which I myself selected."

The other looked curiously at him, but said nothing

more. Together they leaned upon the rail, looking over the side as the launch bore men to the edge of the ice. The men leaped out, scrambled onto the ice, and carried the dead seals to the launch.

Idly Agtuk fingered his knife. Truly the men on the ship had miraculous weapons, but it would be no honor to meet Kalak with such a thing. He turned a dubious gaze on the other Eskimo.

"With my own eyes have I seen much which I would not have believed real if I had not seen it," he stated. "Yet, I would feel much more at ease were I in a kayak."

"Why?"

"There is going to be a great storm."

"The ship is seaworthy."

"That may be, but I am not handling it."

"Can you handle a kayak in a storm?"

"During a storm on the Bay of Seals," Agtuk said quietly, "I capsized many times before I finally reached shore, but I did reach it. It was nothing which most of the men of the Endorah could not repeat. It would be best if you warn the man who handles this ship that there will be a great storm."

"He knows. He has things which tell him. The ship is safe."

The Eskimo left him to go forward, and the ship went on up the lead, mile after mile.

Natkus crouched by his master, watching suspiciously the men who passed them on the deck. The big dog did not like these cramped quarters, and often gazed toward the ice. Agtuk stooped to scratch his ears. Breath-taking though they might be, ships such as this were not for himself and his dog.

Suddenly Natkus pricked up his ears, whimpered, and trotted forward along the narrow deck. The big dog's tail was stiff. He bristled, and a low growl bubbled from his throat.

Agtuk followed him softly. There was something up ahead of the ship and Natkus had smelled it. A little thrill of anticipation fluttered through Agtuk. He had come to find and to fight Kalak, the mist bear. She could not be very far away unless, of course, she had travelled so far and so fast that she was already deep in the ice fields that must begin where this water ended. If that were so, then Agtuk would have to take leave of the ship and penetrate the ice to search for her.

The ship rounded an elbow bend where the lead narrowed. Directly beneath him, almost under the bows, Agtuk saw Kalak and her swimming cubs.

The ship was almost upon her before Kalak knew of its presence. The wind had been blowing from her to the *Narwhal,* and she did not see it until it rounded the elbow bend. It was too late to return to the safety of the ice they had just left. By now they were more than halfway across the lead. It was better to go on than to turn back.

Kalak swam so strongly that she left the weaker cubs two lengths behind her. She swerved away from the steep ice ridge toward which she had been swimming and cut toward a gentle slope where the cubs could crawl out easily. Then she circled and came up behind the cubs.

The mother bear bunted them with her nose, and whined anxiously as she kept her ears attuned to the sounds behind her. This was the danger she feared most, the one against which she knew no defense.

A sudden wind snarled across the water, kicking up choppy waves. The ice she had just left began to grind and crack as it started to break up. The storm was coming up fast, making progress more difficult for the desperately swimming cubs.

Kalak heard the sputtering launch cut away and approach. Deliberately she dropped farther behind the cubs. Even though she did not know how to fight such a thing, she would try. The cubs drew away, nearer the ice every second.

Kalak turned to swim straight at the launch, snarling in fury. Of the six men who rode in it, the bear recognized only Agtuk. She raised herself as high as she could in the water, once more ready to come to grips with her old enemy. With her eye Kalak judged the distance from the waterline to the launch's deck, and calculated just how far she would have to spring in order to reach it. Just as she was ready to leap, the launch swerved to one side. A rope snaked out, the loop settled about her neck, and the launch sputtered on.

The bear tried to bend her head so she could bite the choking thing about her throat, and flailed wildly with her front paws. Even though she had to pull the rope tighter to do so, she turned far enough to see the cubs scramble up the slope and disappear among the ice hummocks. They had escaped; now she could give all of her time to fighting.

She tried to swim toward the launch, and it again swerved out of her way. Choking snarls rattled through her constricted throat as she clawed at the tightening rope. A great wave, blown by the fast-heightening wind, rolled over her head. When she surfaced again, she discovered that, somehow, another rope had settled around her front paw. The launch moved toward the ship, towing her relentlessly along through the succession of waves that rolled in.

Kalak was dragged under again, and when the slackening ropes finally permitted her to rise she could only sputter through the water in her mouth and lungs. They were beside the ship, she discovered, and the ropes which held her had been thrown up to the *Narwhal's* deck. Kalak turned to reckon with this new enemy.

She scraped ineffectively at the *Narwhal's* hull, trying to climb it. She could not, and when the ship leaned heavily toward her in the swell, she was again cast beneath the surface.

The ice fields on the other side of the lead were breaking up. Driven by the wind, tossed by high seas, huge chunks of them were pitching about. A man on deck shouted down to those in the launch.

"Rope her hind legs and belly and we'll winch her up!"

"Make it fast!" a man in the launch yelled back. "This storm's building up to heavy weather!"

Still trying to climb the ship's side so she could get at the men on deck, Kalak was almost unaware when the launch crawled up behind her. A heavy rope encircled her hind legs, and was worked about her belly. Another rope tightened about her legs, and the slack was thrown up to the deck.

The winch began to creak. Raging and snarling, but unable to free herself, Kalak was lifted helplessly into the air. She was suspended over the front of a steel cage while the ropes trailing from her neck and paws were drawn through the open door and out the cage's back end. A dozen men grabbed the ropes.

Kalak was lowered to the deck. As soon as her paws touched solid planking she tried to lunge at the nearest group of men. She could not reach them. Slowly, steadily, she was pulled into the cage and held there. The steel door clanged shut. The bolt dropped into place.

Agtuk flamed with anger. With only Natkus for a companion and his own ice-sense as guide, he had travelled many days' journey from the Bay of Seals. He had found Kalak, the mist bear, only to be cheated out of his fight with her by the men on board the ship.

It had been no part of the bargain that they were to have Kalak, that they were to pursue her in their noisy oomiak, truss her up ignominiously, and imprison her

in a steel cage. Agtuk watched her as she bit at the
ropes that still trailed from her paws and body. With
one snap of her jaws she sheared them cleanly in two,
then used her long claws to work off the loops. Agtuk's
rage increased. Kalak was his enemy, and his alone.
Certainly he had not travelled so far to be cheated of
his battle. He could not go back to the Bay of Seals
and tell the villagers that other men had captured Kalak after he found her. Agtuk grasped a line to steady
himself on the pitching ship, and used his other hand
to stop the Eskimo who had first hailed him.

"Let me go!" the other cried. "The ship is in danger!"

"It is not my ship," Agtuk said, "and who are you to
go when a chief would speak with you? Why have
they imprisoned Kalak?"

"I do not know! Let me go!"

"Kalak is my game," Agtuk continued. "I do not
wish to fight anyone unless I must, but I have my bow,
my lance, and my knife. Unless Kalak is freed, and
put back on the ice, I am going to attack the ship."

"You are mad!" the other cried. "Can you not see
what the storm is doing to the ship?"

"I can see, but the ship is not my worry. Unless it
will weather storms, whoever brought it here should

not have done so. Go now, and deliver my message."

Agtuk released him. Stumbling, steadying himself against the rail, the other disappeared in the spray that was dashing over the deck.

The ship had fought its way around the elbow bend to the wider part of the lead but, in spite of all it could do, the screaming wind still drove it steadily toward the ice. Agtuk's gaze roved along the line of ice, and he selected the probable point at which the *Narwhal* would strike. He stooped to gather his weapons.

Agtuk knew this sea, for he had lived his whole life upon it, and he was not afraid. There was no storm which he could not weather once he was upon the ice. And he would be there soon.

A split second before the *Narwhal* crashed against the ice barrier, Agtuk stooped to pull the pin that locked Kalak's cage. Then he and Natkus leaped over the side.

As the ship struck, a great crashing rose above the wild wind and the grinding ice. The *Narwhal* bounced away and smashed again, but Agtuk and Natkus scrambled farther up the ice as soon as they landed. Agtuk turned to see Kalak come over the side and drop within ten feet of them. The battered ship lurched out toward open water.

Agtuk paid no further attention to it, for now there was only one thing to occupy him. Natkus left his side and, like the expert bear hunter he was, dived at Kalak's flank. His lance poised, Agtuk went in.

Half a ton of cat-quick fury, Kalak charged. She had learned something about lances and, quick as Agtuk was, she was quicker. She sideslid when he thrust. Agtuk saw his lance clatter to the ground and thought of his bow, but there was no time now to nock an arrow. He drew his knife.

Kalak's charge bore him to the ice as easily as if he had been a baby. But, even as he went down, Agtuk thrust and slashed, rolling on his side. Dazed, he struggled to his feet. He and Natkus were alone.

The mist bear was gone, melted into the gloom which had gathered thickly on the heels of the storm. Agtuk looked at the fistful of white hair he clutched in his hand, and back into the mist. He smiled. He had had his battle. It had not been much of a fight, for the bear had merely knocked him out of the way in her hurry to find her cubs. Still, he had fought Kalak with a knife, and the fur was his token to prove that. From this time on Agtuk's rule of the village would be secure. He knew in his own mind that he was fit to be Chief. He also knew that Chuesandrin could never make a charm to overcome the might of a man who dared fight Kalak at close range.

Agtuk began his long journey home.

A mile and a half from the place where they had climbed upon the ice, Kalak found her disconsolate cubs. They rushed gladly to her, whimpering with joy, and Kalak nosed each one gently. Then she turned north. The inaccessible ice fields were only a little distance away; they should reach them tonight. She had taken her babies to safety and this time she would keep them safe until they were grown and able to fend for themselves.

Kalak headed into the thickening mist.

THE AUTHOR

Although Jim Kjelgaard likes to have his name pronounced in the Danish way, Kyell'-gard, his boyhood was as American as Tom Sawyer's. A great grandson of the man who brought the family name from Denmark, he was born in New York City in 1910, but grew up on a mountain farm in the famous Black Forest region of Pennsylvania. Here, surrounded by forest-covered mountains cut by game trails and trout streams, he and his four brothers lived a rugged, outdoor life, and grew up wise in the ways of the woods. The year he graduated from high school, Jim and an-

other boy spent a season on their own in the wilderness, hunting and trapping.

Jim's greatest interests have always been the out-of-doors, animals, and American history, and he has written about all three. Forest Patrol *describes the adventures of a young forest ranger.* Rebel Siege *is a tale of frontier life during the Revolution.* Big Red *is a story of a boy and a champion Irish setter in the wilderness.* Buckskin Brigade *tells of the frontiersmen who led the way across the continent.* Snow Dog *describes the life of a dog on his own in the wilderness.*

Jim Kjelgaard now makes his home in Milwaukee, from which he and his equally outdoor wife make as many expeditions to the wilds as possible. Small daughter Karen can't quite keep up with her parents yet, but she's learning fast.